ST LOUIS AFFAIR

THE ADVENTURES OF HERBERT FALKEN

MICHAEL SCHEFFEL

Other books by Michael Scheffel

Storm on the Horizon

Published by Michael Scheffel Publishing
Copyright © 2015 Michael Scheffel

www.michaelscheffel.com

Printed by Lightning Source

Cover design and book formatting by BookCoverCafe.com

ISBN:
978-0-9906641-5-4 (pbk)
978-0-9906641-6-1 (ebk)

ACKNOWLEDGMENTS

It is said that no man is an island. I feel this is especially true for an indie author. It is my name on the cover, but many others have freely contributed their time, effort, and encouragement to the finished product. I owe this support staff, for lack of a better term, a debt of gratitude that can never be fully repaid.

First and foremost, I want to thank my partner, Christine Gage. She quietly endures the long hours I spend in my other world, for weeks and months at a time. Sometimes I forget to tell her that I appreciate her understanding and patience.

To Martin Andrews, stepfather and dear friend, thank you for your technical expertise and advice.

I also owe a big thank-you to Christine, Gina Briganti and Mance Miller for critiquing the manuscript. I appreciate your time, thoughtful comments and suggestions.

To the team at Book Cover Cafe: Anthony, Penny and Kelly, I am grateful for your outstanding work.

Finally, I offer kudos to the folks at Literature & Latte for their brilliant creations: Scrivener, and Scapple. I cannot imagine trying to write without these applications.

CHAPTER ONE

Head ringing, Herbert Falken dodged left on wobbly legs. Another meaty fist smashed into his right cheek, sending spittle flying and blurring his vision. Immediately the other fist smacked into his ribcage, sending a stab of pain straight through him. Any retreat was cut off by another blow to the ribs and a short punch to the solar plexus. Wincing and gasping, vision narrowing, he lurched forward and threw his arms around his larger adversary's sweaty, bare-skinned torso. Pinning the man's arms to his sides, Falken hung on, struggling to breathe, and tried to blink the stars out of his eyes.

The crowd roared and howled in the smoky, dimly lit warehouse. A cacophony of voices—excited, panicked, angry, lustful, disgusted—reverberated off stacks of shipping barrels and crates.

One drunken voice called out, "This is a fight, not a dance. Get on with it."

Others rang out:

"Fight!"

"Take his head off!"

"Kill him!"

The large man twisted and turned in an effort to break the clinch and free his massive arms, but Falken was not ready to let go; another flurry like the last might finish him. He had to gather his wits and wait for the right moment.

As the catcalls and jeers continued, a few rowdy spectators expressed their impatience by slinging beer at the fighters. Some threw handfuls of dirt scooped up from the floor, and others who were within range spit tobacco juice and phlegm at the struggling pair.

Insult piled on insult caused the large man to growl, snort and thrash like an enraged bull. He surged right, left, forward and backward, squirming and flexing in an attempt to break Falken's hold. With every passing second, his anger swelled.

Finally he roared, *"Let go of me!"*

A man jumped up on a hogshead and yelled, "If you won't knock him out, I will." Then he threw an empty beer bottle.

Falken located the voice, saw the cocked arm moving forward, and twisted sideways. When the bottle hit the back of the bull's head with a dull *thunk*, Falken knew his moment had arrived. He raised his head, exposing his face, and waited.

Red-faced and eyes boiling with hate, the large man craned his neck backward, then snapped his head forward and down. At the last moment, Falken dropped his chin. He felt and heard the cartilage break as the bull's nose smashed into the top of his head. He released his grip and looked up.

The bull was stumbling backward, howling in pain as blood poured from his twisted nose. In that moment, Falken did not see the bull standing before him; his mind superimposed hellish images of his stepfather and Colonel Hawkins.

Pitiless, Falken advanced and attacked with hate-fueled rage. He followed two quick left jabs to the ruined nose with a sharp right to the belly.

Disoriented and deflated, the bull dropped both arms to protect his middle, and reeled backward. Falken stepped in and, with every ounce of energy left, planted a right uppercut on his opponent's chin. The massive head snapped up and back, and the large man collapsed.

The crowd exploded with exclamations, expletives, whistles, flailing arms, and pointing fingers. Beer and whiskey sloshed out of bottles and tin cups. Jaws dropped and eyes were wide with disbelief.

After pausing several seconds to be sure the other man was finished, Falken turned away. He walked over to one of the barrels marking the perimeter of the ad-hoc boxing ring, and reclaimed the coarse gray shirt and flat cap he had left there. Buttoning up, he ignored the hands patting him on the shoulder and the congratulatory voices. He did not fight for adulation; guilt, unrequited vengeance, and the thrill of battle motivated him.

Dressed, he pulled a rag from his hip pocket, wiped blood off his face and knuckles, and pushed through the crowd.

The working-class men were clustered in small groups, stinking of sweat, stale beer and cheap whiskey. A few middle-class gents, distinguished by their inexpensive suits and bowler hats, milled about singly and in pairs, drinking from flasks. Wagers were settled, while new ones were placed on the next fight.

After a few minutes of winding through the throng, Falken spotted a cluster of men under a green-shaded lantern hanging from a roof support. He walked up to the man in the center of the group and held out his hand, palm up.

Seamus O'Donnell—jacket off, vest half unbuttoned, and shirtsleeves rolled up—removed his bowler and mopped sweat from his brow with a soiled handkerchief. His wrinkled face furrowed. "I'll never understand it," he said. "Makes no sense at all. That beast should've broken you up for kindling."

Falken wasn't sure if O'Donnell was sweating freely because of the humid summer air, or the pile of cash he was paying out. Few had been willing to lay any wagers on Falken until the odds had been raised to five to one. It made sense. A sound strategy and the patience to execute it would always best brute force.

The bookmaker snorted and spat. Then, brow furrowed even deeper, he reached into the carpetbag at his feet and withdrew a worn leather pouch. With another snort, he shook out five double eagles—one hundred dollars—and slapped the gold coins into Falken's waiting palm.

"It was blind luck, nothing more. I'll find a beast to put you under, and it'll be a glorious night when I do."

Falken pocketed his winnings and turned away with a smug grin.

With aching ribs, stinging face and sore hands, Herbert Falken pedaled his bicycle away from the Victor Street warehouse on St Louis' south side. The cycle bumped and thumped over the uneven paving bricks, jarring him. He could have come in on the electric trolley from his Tower Grove home in the sprawling city's western section, but he preferred to cycle when he could.

He didn't own a carriage or horse. Though a skilled rider, he felt a horse was an expensive nuisance for a city dweller. The animals required constant care and a steady supply of fodder, from which an equally steady supply of manure was produced. Space for even a small stable would have required purchasing another lot, or sacrificing a sizable portion of his fledgling garden.

Automobiles fascinated Falken, yet he remained unsure about the wisdom of buying one. The noisy machines seemed plagued by mechanical breakdowns and didn't seem to motor along much faster than he could pedal. So he used the bicycle, time and weather permitting; otherwise, the trolley lines served his transportation needs.

Coasting to a stop at Carondelet Avenue, a tingle ran down Falken's spine. He twisted around, as much as his aching ribs allowed. He had the feeling he was being watched. He looked up and down the wide thoroughfare, and peered into shadows. A carriage crossed Carondelet a few blocks north; dogs barked near and far; a gentle breeze stirred air heavy with humidity and coal smoke; lightning flashed to the west. The city was asleep, yet he felt eyes upon him.

A voice called out from his right, "What are you doing there?"

Falken tensed and turned toward the sound. An active criminal element preyed on the poor neighborhoods near the levee. He wondered if someone was looking for an easy mark leaving the fights. A smart gang might have put a lookout in the warehouse.

A silhouette appeared out of the nearest alley. "I asked you a question."

Falken relaxed. "Shouldn't you be out clubbing old men and robbing children?"

"Major Falken?"

"And good evening to you, Captain Morrissey."

The shadowy figure stepped into a pool of light under an electric streetlamp. He wore the English-style dark blue tunic with brass buttons, dark blue custodian helmet, and gold, six-pointed star badge of a St. Louis police captain.

"Didn't recognize you in the dark, Major," Morrissey offered.

Many addressed Falken as Major, out of respect, even though he no longer wore his country's uniform. He had gained nationwide notoriety for his part in a brutal campaign against renegade border raiders. Wounded in battle and taken prisoner and tortured, Falken had been celebrated as a hero by newspapers and magazines across the country.

A year later, Falken furthered his fame and inadvertently secured his fortune by ending Kingman's bloody reign of terror. A series of published articles, under his own by line, had chronicled the investigation.

Head and eyes moving, taking in their immediate surroundings, the tall, heavily-built Irishman grinned. "Been to the fights, I see. It's hard to tell from the damage if you won or lost."

Falken felt his right cheek swelling and was certain he would have at least one black eye. There was also a stinging cut below his right eyebrow. "It was close for a while, but the giant went down, as they all do. What brings you out on a Saturday night?"

"Doing my job, checking on the men. It's important for them to know I'm watching. Keeps them on their toes."

"Oh, I thought you might be going down to break up the fights."

"Why? Working men need entertainment. Besides, it'd be bad publicity to arrest a hero. They'd be screaming for my head from City Hall to Vandeventer Place."

"What a shocking statement from a police captain. American justice is blind. We're all equal in the eyes of the law."

"Right, and I'll make you a good deal on Merchants Bridge." Captain Morrissey shook his head, though still grinning. "I don't understand why you do it."

"I need something to do at night."

"There's better ways to pass the time than slumming down here getting your face smashed in, a man with your brains and talents. You sure don't need the money."

Ruby Kingman, devastated by the depth of her husband's evil, had gifted Falken a small fortune "to finance his continued good works." A few days later she took her own life.

"Yours is not to reason why, Captain."

"I suppose not. But maybe I should order a raid. At least I could keep you from getting yourself killed."

Lightning flashes were becoming brighter and more frequent. Dogs yipped and barked in response. The air was getting noticeably heavier.

"I better get going. Looks like a bad one's coming our way," Falken said.

"You do have a ways to go on that thing. And I have business to see to."

Falken pushed off and began pedaling. He said over his shoulder, "Collections for the Widows and Orphans Charity?"

"No, my bookmaker. When my spies reported you were at the warehouse, I put an eagle down on you."

Falken chuckled, and then winced as a deep bass roll of thunder reached his ears.

CHAPTER TWO

*S*creams. *Shrill, tormented, agonizing screams.*

Falken's eyes snapped open, and he sat bolt upright. A sharp jolt of pain sliced through his ribcage and his head pounded. Breathing heavily, bathed in sweat, every muscle drawn taut, he dared not move. He braced for the next blow. A cry caught in his throat. His eyes darted around, searching.

After several tense moments, he recognized his bedroom and relaxed from head to foot. He wanted to collapse back onto his pillow, but the possibility of going back to sleep was worse than the alternative.

As nightmare images faded from his mind's eye, his senses began awakening. Morning brightness seeped around the edges of the heavy draperies. The sheet under his legs felt wet and clammy. A shiver radiated through him, although the house was already warm; someone was moving around downstairs; coffee was brewing.

With grim determination, Falken swung his legs over the side of the canopy bed and parted the filmy silk curtain.

He stood and tested his legs. At least some part of me is functioning normally, he thought. Slowly, he stretched and flexed individual muscle groups, taking inventory of the previous night's damage. The pain was bearable, familiar, perhaps even comforting. He had endured far worse and recovered without permanent disability, despite the opinion of an army medical board.

His pocket watch, on the bedside table, read seven-ten.

At half past seven, Falken descended the main staircase of his spacious home and turned left into the dining room. He was dressed for a leisurely August Sunday: crisp white shirt buttoned to the neck, brown twill trousers with braces, matching socks with garters, and brown low-quarter shoes; each article was creased or polished in military fashion. He took his chair at the head of the white-cloth-covered table, set for two.

The dining room, like the rest of the house, was new and modern: construction had been completed the previous autumn. A fine Persian rug covered mahogany floorboards; alabaster walls rose ten feet, with rich oak baseboards, crown moldings and door trim; an electric crystal chandelier hung from the ceiling; furnishings were sturdy and functional; a print of *Washington Crossing the Delaware* hung on the wall behind him.

Luke Owen entered from the kitchen, carrying a coffee service, and stopped mid-stride, eyes wide. His abrupt halt nearly caused everything to slide off the silver tray. He jerked backward and managed to keep his load balanced, though just barely. The twenty-two-year-old former infantryman had only been with Falken for two months, but he knew better than to comment on his employer's appearance.

"Mr. Westfall," Owen announced loudly enough to be heard in the next room, and continued with his task. He placed two bone-china cups on the table, and filled them with steaming coffee from a silver pot. Then he arranged the pot, sugar bowl and creamer within reach of both place settings.

James Westfall limped out of the parlor and crossed the hallway into the dining room. Focused on a copy of the *Post-Dispatch*, he rounded the table and pulled out his customary chair on Falken's right before looking up. After a moment, he said, "Major, not again."

Falken had permitted himself to skip shaving, but he had seen his face in the mirror. His right cheek was red and swollen, as was the eye above. His left jawline, temple and neck bore deep red marks. A bushy brown handlebar mustache concealed his puffy upper lip.

Falken turned to Owen, who stood on his left, waiting. "I'll have four hard-fried eggs, four strips of crisp bacon, a slice of fried ham, and two lightly buttered biscuits. Westfall?"

"The same, with fried potatoes," Westfall said.

Falken added, "Owen, try to not blacken the eggs this time. You must learn breakfast, as I will not ask Mrs. Howard to work on Sunday."

"I'll do my best, Major," Owen replied, and returned to the kitchen.

The young man had proven himself an efficient orderly. He had been discharged from the army after treatment for yellow fever he contracted in Cuba. Owen rarely spoke about his war service, or any other subject. Orphaned young, he seemed wary of personal relationships, but his quiet devotion to Falken was readily apparent.

After a sip of coffee, Falken said, "Anything interesting in the news?"

Westfall stared at Falken for another long moment, frowned, and shook his head. "Mr. Bryan is making speeches, sounding like he intends to run for president again. Colonel—excuse me, *Governor* Roosevelt—is also trumpeting the populist progressive agenda. I suspect he'd also like to sit in the White House."

"I applaud what he did to modernize the navy, and deeply respect his service in Cuba, but that man's ego will be his downfall."

"Downfall?" Westfall snorted. "Sitting there looking like a horse kicked you in the face, *you* forecast another man's downfall? Talk about the pot and kettle."

"Looks far worse than it is. Nothing to worry about."

"I most respectfully disagree, Major. And I won't sit here pretending nothing's happened. I'm calling Dr. Evans." The twenty-five-year-old former cavalry lieutenant dropped the newspaper on the table and stomped out of the room.

"Westfall, come back here and sit down. Dr. Evans doesn't need to be called out on a Sunday morning. Westfall, do you hear me? Westfall?"

Falken heard his aide-de-camp's voice in the hall.

"Operator, connect me with Dr. Rupert Evans, please." ... "Doctor, James Westfall. I'm sorry to trouble you at this hour on Sunday." ... "Yes, Doctor, it appears he has." ... "Thank you, Doctor."

Westfall reentered the dining room, looked at Falken again, grimaced and took his chair. "Dr. Evans will be here within the hour."

Falken sipped his coffee—carefully, as it stung his cut upper lip. He was angry, no, annoyed. Yes, annoyed by Westfall summoning Evans. He wanted to scold the younger man soundly, but knew he would not. Westfall was certainly naive and, at times, downright dense, but he meant well. He had been at Falken's side, playing mother hen, since they had met in the Fort Riley officers' infirmary two and a half years earlier. Both had been facing an unwelcome early end to their military careers, and shared frustrations grew into a bond of friendship and trust.

After several moments of silence, Falken thought perhaps a light reprimand was in order after all. "Disobeying an order is a serious breach of discipline. I would've thought you learned that at West Point."

Westfall replied without contrition. "Major, I was taught that an officer's first duty is to the general welfare of his command, superiors as well as subordinates. I'm simply doing my job."

Falken raised a finger and opened his mouth, but stopped short when Owen pushed through the door with a dish of blackberry jam. Instead of prolonging the debate, Falken reached for his cup and put the matter out of his mind. He was incapable of being cross with Westfall for long. The man was like a dutiful younger brother, headstrong yet loyal.

"Breakfast will be ready shortly," Owen said.

At eight o'clock, Westfall limped back into the dining room ahead of Dr. Evans.

Evans made and held eye contact with Falken for a long moment, then turned to Westfall. "Is last night's rain bothering your leg?"

The doctor's scorching gaze left Falken feeling like an errant schoolboy, but he refused to let it show.

"Yes, Doctor," Westfall said. "It's stiff as a board this morning, but there's nothing new about that."

Evans placed his bag on the table and opened it. "Well, that may lessen over time, but it'll always be there in some fashion." Still speaking to Westfall, he locked eyes with Falken again. "Would you finish your breakfast in the kitchen, please?" The white-haired physician carried himself like a man accustomed to having his instructions obeyed.

With a respectful nod to Evans, and a you-are-going-to-get-yours glance at Falken, the younger man picked up his plate and hobbled from the room.

While arranging the tools of his trade, Evans snapped, "Herbert, why do you do this to yourself? Pawing the ground, beating your chest, and brawling like a mindless ape. My god, you look awful. I don't know why I waste my time treating you. Give me your hands."

Evans pressed, pulled and wiggled Falken's fingers, then dabbed disinfectant on his swollen, scraped knuckles.

"Men have died down there, been literally beaten to death. And for what? Sport? Glory? A few dollars? It's simply insane to risk your life so carelessly for so little. Yet you do it time and again. Are you seeking an early death? Raise your arms and put your hands on top of your head."

Falken did so slowly, wincing with the effort. He had only known Evans for a couple of years, but the good doctor was the closest he had ever come to having a genuine father figure in his life. Evans, like Westfall, had offered Falken friendship at the lowest point of his life, when he had needed it most. Both men knew about his parents, Anna, and the real story of Colonel Hawkins. He had always given them the unvarnished truth.

Falken chose his words carefully. "Many men seek solace from liquor. Others choose opium. Some look to money. I'm not one of these. For better or worse, I am a soldier. Fighting is what I do best. It's what I'm supposed to do, what I *have* to do."

"Oh, rubbish. This is eighteen hundred and ninety-nine. You are a thirty-six-year-old *former* soldier, with the whole world at your feet. You have the intellect of a scholar, the instincts of a hunter, and an iron will. You could succeed at anything."

"I am succeeding."

"Again, rubbish." Evans applied liniment to Falken's right cheek and eye. "Has your work taught you nothing? Look what you did to Kingman. You destroyed that monster with this"—he tapped a finger to his temple—"not your fists. Take your shirt off."

Falken struggled to do as the doctor asked.

"Did bare-knuckle brawling pay for this house?" Evans continued, examining Falken's bruised ribs. "Your staff? Has it gained you the respect and admiration of this city? Does Harper's pay you for boxing tales?"

Falken replied with defiant silence.

Evans sighed, and changed tack. "I've known a few soldiers in my time, and endured my share of battlefields. Do you think Grant won the war by shouldering a rifle and standing on the firing line? Of course not. He won it by outmaneuvering Johnston, Pemberton, Bragg and Lee at every turn. On the other hand, Custer charged into battle consumed by maniacal visions of glory and bloodlust, and where is he now?" Rubbing liniment into the bruised ribs, he concluded his lecture. "It takes the brainpower of a turnip to stand toe to toe and slug it out. Genius, however, is required to lay a man low without lifting a finger. You have that ability; I've seen it. And you can go on fighting with your mind a lot longer than with your body. You can also do yourself and the world more good that way."

Evans began packing up his equipment. "Put your shirt back on. I didn't feel any broken bones, but you're going to hurt for a few days. I can only pray that this time the pain will teach you something."

Falken put his shirt back on. "I often think death would be a relief. But it's not in my nature to give up. I will not let myself be beaten to death."

"But if it happens, so be it? Herbert, think of what you risk throwing away. Life is a most precious gift."

Falken did not respond.

With visible effort, Evans calmed himself. He pulled out a chair and sat, making eye contact. "Still not sleeping?"

Falken shook his head.

"The body heals faster than the soul. I don't have a prescription for putting the past to rest. You have to find that within yourself. But a little whiskey before bed might help you sleep more peacefully."

Falken shook his head. "You know better."

"Well then, find something constructive to occupy your mind. Take on more cases by advertising your investigative services. Write more articles for publication. Design another home. Just stay away from the fighting pits. Anger and despair breed more of the same."

As Falken opened his mouth to reply, the gate buzzer sounded faintly from the kitchen. "Who could that be?"

Westfall made his way down the hall as fast as his game leg allowed and opened the door. A few moments later he escorted a police sergeant into the dining room.

The sergeant removed his custodian helmet and nodded. "Major Falken, Dr. Evans. Major, Captain Morrissey asks that you come with me, official business."

"What kind of official business, Sergeant?"

The sergeant looked around the room as if the answer could be found there. "There's been a murder, Major."

Falken felt an immediate sense of anticipation, a call to action. Sadness and fatigue cleared from his mind. He stood and called for Owen.

The young orderly appeared from the kitchen. "Sir?"

"Have you brushed my gray suit and polished my new black boots?"

"Yes, Major."

"Good man. Come along, I need a shave and possibly some help dressing." He turned to his aide-de-camp. "Westfall, prepare yourself and find my satchel. You know the one, red leather. It should have everything we need, but take inventory to be sure."

Falken looked at Evans. "Doctor, will you join us?"

"My wife will give me hell for missing church, but yes, I think I will," Evans replied with a knowing smile.

CHAPTER THREE

The sergeant stopped the police carriage on the levee next to Eads Bridge among a cluster of carriages and horses, all in police department livery. A dozen patrolmen had formed a line to keep the growing crowd back. Photographers stood by their tripod cameras waiting for a newsworthy shot. Notepads in hand, reporters shouted questions at the stoic patrolmen and new arrivals. The St. Louis Cathedral, to the south, rose majestically among riverfront warehouses, merchant houses and tenements.

The men stepped down from the carriage, except Falken. He stared at the bridge. Chills ran through his body, taking his breath away. He was fixated, unable to look away, unable to move.

"Major? Major Falken? Major Falken?"

"Y-y ... yes?"

"This way if you please, Major," said the sergeant.

Falken forced his eyes away, breaking the spell. He glanced at his companions.

Evans and Westfall stood waiting, eyes downcast and expressions neutral. The sergeant shifted from one foot to the other.

As Falken dismounted, a reporter across the street shouted, "Major Falken! Major, is another madman running loose in the city?"

The question was a reference to the Kingman affair. For three years, Josiah Kingman, a prominent and respected merchant, had terrorized the city. He had preyed on unwary young women, mimicking the killing style of London's Jack the Ripper. Falken had become unofficially involved when he accompanied the doctor to one of the murder scenes. Falken had analyzed the long string of cases and identified patterns of behavior, all of which had led to Kingman's arrest, conviction and hanging. A series of articles published in Harper's *New Monthly* Magazine, detailing the case, had enhanced his folk hero image.

Falken ignored a flurry of shouted questions and exclamations. He did not need another distraction.

"The body's down at the riverbank," the sergeant said, leading the way.

The trio trailed behind him, with Falken in the lead, and Westfall limping along at the rear with the aid of his cane. After crossing the riverfront rail lines, Falken hesitated at the edge of the levee. A large group of policemen were milling around below, at the foot of the massive western bridge abutment.

Evans squeezed Falken's right shoulder. "You're needed here. Focus on the task at hand."

Falken took a deep breath and descended to the riverbank.

Captain Morrissey saw him and winked. "What happened to you, Major? Take a tumble from that bicycle of yours?" A round of half suppressed chuckles accompanied the greeting.

The captain greeted Evans. "Glad you're here, Doctor." He turned to the sergeant. "Weiss, tell headquarters that Dr. Evans is on the scene."

The sergeant nodded and trudged back up the levee.

"Thank you, Captain. I'm always happy to offer my meager services to the police." Evans gave Falken a gentle nudge.

"What do you have here?" Falken asked Morrissey.

"An expensively dressed dead man. We don't know who it is, or what happened. But a corpse in a tailored suit and thirty-dollar shoes is sure to draw attention from City Hall, so I've ordered that nothing be touched. I wanted you to see the body as it was found." Morrissey stepped aside, revealing the corpse.

Falken lost his breath again. The image of another body positioned in the same manner and location flashed into his mind.

"Are you all right, Major? You look like you've seen a ghost," Morrissey said.

Falken closed his eyes, forced himself to inhale, and cleared his mind. *Not now. I answer to you in the dark, but not now.* The image faded, replaced by the call to action. He opened his eyes and walked forward, oblivious to a dozen pairs of staring eyes. He moved in an arc, staying well clear of the corpse. He took his time, studying the ground.

"Who found him?"

"A fisherman in a boat spotted the body, came ashore, and reported to a mounted patrolman," Morrissey said.

"Westfall, do a rough sketch," Falken said. "Don't worry about scale, but note the body's position and general spatial relationships. Captain, is there any reason to believe the fisherman is more than just an observant citizen?"

"None that I can see," Morrissey said, "but I'm holding him, if you have any questions."

Falken nodded, pulled out a monogrammed silk handkerchief, removed his favorite black homburg, and mopped his brow. Only a few clouds remained from the overnight thunderstorm. The morning sun was heating air thick with humidity. An eastbound locomotive chugged, hissed and clattered across the bridge overhead. The shriek of a steam whistle reached his ears from East St. Louis.

Homburg back on his head and handkerchief pocketed, he studied the corpse while Westfall drew a diagram. There were no shoe prints in the immediate area; the investigating patrolman had walked over the ground where Falken stood. The dead man had been extraordinarily tall and carried considerable girth. The body was facedown; arms, head and upper torso were in the water; splayed legs pointed toward the levee. The granite-block abutment anchoring the bridge to the west riverbank was several feet to the left. Foul-smelling, muddy water swirled under the bridge.

"How did he get here?" Falken asked Morrissey.

"Dumped in upstream, floated down here, and the pier eddy washed him up on the bank. It's happened before," the captain said.

"Or the wake of a passing steamboat pushed him onto the bank," Westfall said. "I've finished the sketch, Major."

His new boots sinking into river mud, Falken backed up onto firmer ground. "All right, Captain, pull him out of there."

In response to hand signals from Morrissey, four burly policemen came forward. Two stepped into the water and hooked an arm under each shoulder. The other pair each took hold of an ankle. Together, they grunted and half carried, half dragged the dead man ashore. They dropped their load at Falken's feet with a squishy splat. As the other men came closer, they bent down and rolled the paunchy corpse onto its back.

On seeing the face, Captain Morrissey said, "Holy Mother of God. It's Alderman Garrett."

Falken also recognized the ash-gray face. Charles Garrett was, or had been, a north-side alderman. He had also been a successful businessman. His holdings included a brewery, glassworks, cooperage, cartage company, forestry land, and a majority interest in a small steamboat line. Garrett Lager was a popular brand in the city and surrounding counties.

"Doctor, would you care to examine the deceased?" Morrissey said.

As Evans closed in and knelt, Falken said, "Westfall, take notes."

Evans began by rolling the head from side to side. "He was struck on the left side of the head with a blunt object. More than one blow. I see something …" He pulled a large magnifying glass from a leather satchel and studied the head wound. "A *wooden* blunt object. There are splinters embedded in the scalp."

Moving his hands down the neck and outward, he continued. "Left clavicle is fractured. And so is the left ulna." He opened the bloodstained suit jacket, vest and shirt. Using scissors, he split the undershirt, exposing the flabby chest and abdomen.

More than one veteran policeman groaned at the sight.

"I count eleven, no, thirteen stab wounds," Evans said. "Five in the chest and eight in the abdomen." He used the magnifier again. "Looks like a narrow thin blade, a skinner or fillet knife maybe." He took a surgical probe from his bag and inserted it in several of the wounds. "Both lungs are punctured, as well as the liver." Continuing down the body to the ankles, he added, "Both legs are broken, the left in two places, the right in three. The right femur is protruding through the skin."

"Jesus, Mary and Joseph," Morrissey said, "that's one hell of a beating, and a stabbing on top of it."

"A savage, sadistic beating," Falken agreed. "Cause of death, Doctor?"

"I can't say for certain without an internal examination. But based on what I see, blood loss, probably from the liver. The next best possibility is bleeding into the lungs. I didn't feel any skull fractures, nor see brain matter seeping out, so I don't believe the head wounds were fatal."

Westfall cleared his throat.

"Yes, Westfall?" Falken said.

"Could the bones have been broken if he was run over by a steamboat and thrashed by a sidewheel?"

"Not likely," Morrissey said. "When that happens the clothing's usually shredded. No, this was done by a beast of a man, a real lunatic."

Falken gestured over his shoulder. "You should be careful saying that. The press boys up there don't know anything yet, but they're already trying to draw a parallel with Kingman."

"Christ, that's all I need. Those vultures will sink their claws in and City Hall will start pushing."

Evans grasped his bag, stood and stepped back.

Falken squatted and looked at Garrett closely. After a moment, he said, "I don't see a watch fob." He shifted forward and patted pockets. Then he turned every pocket out. "No watch, wallet, keys, coins, nothing. Mr. Garrett was fully dressed and presumably away from home at the time of death. What man leaves home with empty pockets?"

"His personal items could've fallen out while he was in the river," Westfall offered.

"One or two things possibly, but not every article from every pocket," Falken said. "No, these things were taken by the murderer."

"This is a wagonload of violence for a simple robbery," Morrissey said.

"Exactly. A street robber would have bashed him in the head, rifled his pockets and run away." Falken pointed at the body. "A lone criminal wouldn't have done this and then risked detection by moving him. And he couldn't possibly have carried him. Even a gang would've struggled mightily and created a good deal of noise doing so. Most unlikely, in my opinion."

"So did they use a wagon or carriage?" Westfall asked.

"Westfall, think man, think. Petty thugs don't usually have those at hand. And again, stealing one would involve unnecessary risk. No, this wasn't an ordinary crime."

"Then we're back to a lunatic murderer," Morrissey said. "Damnation." He turned to his lieutenant. "Get the undertaker down here. Make sure you keep the body covered, and not a word about this to anyone. If anything discussed here gets out, I'll hold all of you responsible." He glared at each of his men to reinforce the order. "Right, get it done."

The lieutenant barked orders and policemen began moving.

Falken stood and asked Morrissey, "Shall we accompany you to the Garrett residence?"

"Yes, Major, I want you to come along. You can bring your man, if you wish," Morrissey said, looking at Westfall.

Falken turned to Evans. "Doctor, if you can spare the time?"

"Yes, you may need me," Evans said. "I've been attending the Garrett family since their first child. Margaret's prone to fainting when her emotions are stirred."

A lone policeman stood guard over Garrett's corpse, and the quartet started up the levee.

A train chugged south along the tracks, and a sidewheeler churned its way upstream. Engineer and captain exchanged greetings with double steam-whistle blasts.

CHAPTER FOUR

The black police carriage creaked to a stop at the end of a private north-side street. The pair of horses shook heads and swished their tails at flies.

It was late morning, and the affluent residents, in gleaming carriages and motorcars, were returning from church. Domestic staff, depending on individual position, rode with their employers or walked. A backfiring, stuttering, lurching, open-carriage St. Louis came down the street belching clouds of exhaust and frightening the horses. The driver, goggled and gloved, seemed to be struggling with the steering tiller.

All eyes, however, ignored the spectacle and focused on the police vehicle. Children pointed, parents exchanged questioning glances, and servants whispered to each other.

Stepping out of the mud-splattered police carriage, Falken was impressed with the neighborhood, and the Garrett residence in particular. The three-story, slate-roofed, balconied, brick and stone mansion, fronted by a well-tended lawn, was situated fifty feet back from the street. Granite steps and a flagstone walkway, bordered by electric lampposts, led to a limestone portico and arched double door. A pair of flagstone driveways disappeared behind the house on either side. Oak, maple and hickory trees provided afternoon shade.

Falken noted that none of the properties in the street were walled or fenced in any way, and remarked on the oddity.

"No need for walls and gates here," Morrissey said. "The man at the end of the street who waved us past is part of a team of watchmen paid by the homeowners. They'll bash the brains of anyone caught trespassing, and the burglars know it."

"Too bad Mr. Garrett wasn't attended by one of those brain bashers last night," Westfall said.

"Come along, gentlemen, let us do our unfortunate duty," Evans said, and led the way up the walkway to the portico. Flanked by Morrissey and Falken, with Westfall two steps behind, Evans pressed the door buzzer.

A smartly dressed, middle-aged butler opened the heavy left-hand door. "Dr. Evans, how may I help you?" He eyed the others with open curiosity.

"Adams, we must speak with Margaret."

"You're always welcome, Doctor, but"—Adams stared at Morrissey—"who are these gentlemen?"

Gesturing to his right, Evans said, "Captain Morrissey," then to the left, "Mr. Falken."

Falken pulled out his wallet, withdrew a card and handed it to the butler.

Adams studied the card with interest. "And the other gentleman?" he asked Falken.

"Mr. Westfall, my aide," Falken replied.

"Please come inside, gentlemen," Adams said, pulling both doors fully open.

After Westfall had hobbled through and removed his hat, the butler closed the doors and ushered them through the reception hall into the formal sitting room used for receiving guests.

"Doctor, I will inform Mrs. Garrett of your request. Mr. Garrett is not present at the moment, but he is expected within the hour."

As the starchy butler strode out of the room, Falken took it all in. The architecture, carved woodwork, imported furnishings and European artwork all bespoke refined elegance. In comparison to his own distinctly American tastes, he observed that the Garretts preferred Old World decadence. If it was European, rich people loved it. He had never understood the obsession. He was studying a lesser-known Vermeer when the butler reentered the room.

"Gentlemen, Mrs. Garrett."

A graceful, expensively dressed brunette a few years older than Falken glided into the room. Her green silk dress with white lace collar and cuffs rustled softly. She wore a silver and pearl brooch, and a simple wedding band.

She greeted Evans. "Rupert, whatever brings you here on a Sunday? No one here sent for you." She glanced around. "And why is this policeman with you?"

Two girls in their late teens, Garrett's daughters, walked in and stood behind their mother. They too were attired in silk and lace, although their dresses were cut in a more modern style. With fear in her eyes, the girl who appeared to be the elder daughter of the two looked at Falken and Captain Morrissey.

"Margaret, I want you to sit down," Evans said.

"Sit? Rupert, don't be melodramatic, it's unbecoming."

"Margaret, I have something very important to tell you, and I want you to sit down to hear it."

A young blonde, wearing the black dress, white apron, and white lace headpiece of a parlormaid, appeared in the doorway. "Excuse me, Madam," she said with a noticeable Bavarian accent.

Falken noted her vague resemblance to Anna, and his thoughts drifted. He blinked away a slideshow of terrible mental images. *I can't fall apart every time I see a woman who looks like her,* he told himself. *Stop this.*

Mrs. Garrett turned. "Yes, Gretchen?"

"Mrs. Tolliver asks if your guests will be joining you for dinner."

Mrs. Garrett turned back to Evans. "Rupert, you and your companions are most welcome at our table. We will be seated as soon as Charles returns, and I insist that you dine with us. Gretchen, tell Mrs. Tolliver we have four guests, then bring these gentlemen iced tea and—"

"Mother," the elder daughter snapped, "stop being a gracious hostess and hear what Dr. Evans has to say. It's something dreadful."

Falken was roused from his trance by her outburst. She seemed to be staring through him. She pointed at him with her chin. "That one looks as though he's attending a funeral."

"Ruth! Apologize this—"

Evans seized the moment. "Margaret," he said. He grasped Mrs. Garrett's shoulders with both hands. "Margaret, Charles is not coming home. I'm deeply sorry to tell you he's no longer with us."

"Rupert, whatever are you talking about? Charles will be here—"

Evans cut her off. "Charles is dead."

Mrs. Garrett stiffened, but remained silent. Jaw quivering, she closed her eyes.

Ruth continued staring at Falken without seeing him, while her sister gasped and clutched her midriff.

The parlormaid's expression switched from servile indifference to horror. Her eyes filled with tears as she crossed her arms and muttered, *"Mein Gott ein Himmel."*

The butler took a step back, sagged against the doorjamb, and bowed his head.

Still staring blankly at Falken, Ruth said, "Are you certain my father is dead?"

"Yes," he said.

The younger girl cried out, doubled over, and dropped to her knees. The startled butler recovered his composure, and rushed over to help her to an armchair. He went down on one knee and embraced the wailing teenager. Shoulders shaking, the parlormaid held her face with both hands and sobbed.

"Who are you?" Ruth asked Falken without inflection.

"Herbert Falken."

"Ah, the famous Major Falken." Ruth turned to Morrissey. "If Major Falken is here, then you believe father was murdered."

Morrissey looked at the floor. "I'm sorry, miss."

The younger daughter threw back her head back and screeched, "Daaaddddyyyy!" She resumed her anguished wailing.

The maid backed into the reception hall and fled toward the back of the house.

Mrs. Garrett wavered and collapsed. Evans had been ready and caught her. "Herbert, help me."

Forcing a final distant memory back into its hidden recess, Falken moved. Together, they carried the murmuring widow to an antique sofa. Her head lolled on a brocade cushion and she called softly to her husband.

Evans retrieved his bag and withdrew a bottle of smelling salts. "Ruth, sit with your sister and comfort her. I'll examine her after I finish with your mother." He turned to the butler. "Adams, these gentlemen need to speak with you privately. Be frank with them. They have my friendship and confidence."

The butler pressed his handkerchief into the distraught younger girl's hand, stood and straightened his jacket. He nodded to Evans, then led the way across the hall to the gentlemen's parlor.

The room's high walls were decorated with game trophies from all over North America and northern Europe. A brown bear stood in the near left corner, jaws open and claws extended. Carved walnut gun cabinets flanked the fireplace, displaying an ample collection of long guns and handguns. Overstuffed leather chairs formed a quadrangle in the center of the room atop a dark deep-pile rug; each chair was flanked by a small round table and ornate ashtray.

As the butler was closing the double doors, a matronly woman approached with a questioning expression.

"Feed the boys," Adams told her, "then take them out to play in the garden. Keep them away from the front rooms. I'll explain later."

With concerned eyes, the woman nodded and the doors closed.

"Please be seated, gentlemen." The butler crossed to a chair facing the fireplace and sat at attention.

Falken pulled out his leather cigar case, and worked through the process of preparing and lighting one as the others arranged themselves. Morrissey unbuttoned his tunic and mopped his brow. Westfall withdrew a leather-bound journal and Waterman fountain pen from the red-leather satchel.

Cigar tip glowing and his aide ready to record the interview, Falken paced slowly around the room's perimeter. "How many children are there?" he asked Adams.

"Six, two daughters and four sons. The oldest, Ruth, is nineteen. Alfred, the youngest, will be seven next month."

"Staff?"

"Myself, of course, and my wife, the governess. Our son is the stableman and drives the carriage. Then there is the housekeeper, who supervises the cook, kitchenmaid, chambermaid and parlormaid. The housekeeper's husband serves as gardener."

"How long have you been with Garrett?"

"Since we were both in knickers. I started as his valet. My father was butler then."

"So one could assume you knew him well. You could anticipate his needs, read his moods, and so forth?"

"Yes."

"Did you note any unusual behavior lately? Was Garrett acting as though he was troubled by anything?"

Adams abandoned his stiff formal posture and leaned forward, putting his elbows on his knees. He exhaled loudly. "For the past year he has seemed distracted, sullen even."

"Do you know why?"

"He refused to confide in me, but I knew there was ... a grave financial concern."

"Garrett had money problems?"

"Yes. Staff salaries for the month of May weren't paid until mid-June. Everyone received half pay for June in the last week of July. The balance for June, and July's wages, are in arrears. Household accounts at Vandervoort's, and the grocer, butcher and icehouse are also past due. Charles is, or was, usually very prompt about settling accounts."

"Have any of the staff protested?"

"A week ago, the housekeeper gave me notice for herself, her husband, the cook, kitchenmaid and chambermaid. Unless all wages owed are paid by the end of the month, they will leave. My wife and I will stay on, of course, and Gretchen, the parlormaid, is apparently staying as well."

"Your son?"

"He's enlisting in the navy."

"Does Mrs. Garrett know about the resignations?"

"No. Charles told me everyone would be paid, life would return to normal, and there was no need to worry his wife. He never discussed business or money with Mrs. Garrett."

Falken tapped his cigar on the edge of a large crystal ashtray. "Who would know specifics about Garrett's financial difficulties?"

"Keller, the bookkeeper. He maintains the business and personal ledgers. He's in his office at Garrett House every morning by seven-thirty."

Wreathed in a cloud of aromatic smoke, Falken nodded. After a moment, he resumed pacing and continued his questioning. "Did Garrett leave the house last evening?"

"No, he left early, right after breakfast. He said he had business across the river, and intended to remain overnight. He said he would return today in time for dinner. I was expecting him when you arrived."

"Do you know who he intended to meet?"

"In East St. Louis, he was meeting with Vesper, the manager of the breeding stable, Morgan, who oversees the warehouses at the eastside rail yard, and Unger, manager of the sawmill. He said he would then go to Belleville to dine with Mr. Decker and would most likely sleep there. I'm unaware of the context, but he made a habit of going to Belleville two or three times a month."

"Mr. Decker of the Decker Steamboat Line?"

"Yes. He, Charles, and a Mr. Fulton of Memphis are the majority shareholders."

"Are all of the staff present today?"

"No. The housekeeper, gardener and chambermaid have Sunday off. The kitchenmaid reported ill Monday. She's been out all week, and I suspect she's been seeking new employment."

"Does any of the staff reside here?"

"My family, and Gretchen."

"Gretchen, the parlormaid?"

Adams nodded.

"When is Gretchen's day off?"

"Saturday." Adams sat up straight and made eye contact with Falken. "How did Charles die? *Was* he murdered?"

Falken briefly detailed the condition of the corpse, and where and how it was found.

Adams deflated and began weeping. "I can't believe it. Charles was an excellent marksman."

"He left here yesterday armed?"

"Yes. When he was sixteen, Charles was beaten and robbed by a gang of hoodlums. His father gave him a derringer, with instructions to shoot anyone who threatened him. He hasn't gone out of the house without a handgun since."

"What was he carrying?"

"A Model 91 Smith and Wesson."

"Would he have used it?"

Adams stared with incredulity. "Absolutely."

Falken opened his mouth to speak, and glanced at Morrissey. The captain shook his head, and Falken remained silent.

"We use Alexander's in these matters," Morrissey told Adams. "I'll send a messenger when the remains are ready for release to a mortuary of Mrs. Garrett's choosing. Is there anything else, Major?"

Fire in his eyes, Falken stubbed out his cigar in the crystal ashtray and glared at Captain Morrissey. After a long moment, he said, "I may need to speak with the staff individually, but that can wait for now. Thank you, Adams, you have my sympathy." He walked over and squeezed the older man's shoulder.

Westfall packed up the satchel, and Morrissey stood and buttoned up his tunic. Then the trio proceeded to the door.

His hand on the latch, Falken paused and looked at the butler. "Adams, aside from the revolver, what did Garrett usually carry in his pockets when he left the house?"

"His wallet, his watch with a family photograph inside, keys, a handful of gold and silver, cigar case and a flask," Adams replied tearfully.

"Did any of those have an identifying mark?"

"The watch, a gift from his father, is monogrammed. The wallet, cigar case, and flask bear the Garrett House emblem; he had them made several years ago."

Falken nodded, glared at Morrissey again, opened the doors and stepped into the reception hall.

Evans came out of the sitting room. "They're resting, but extreme emotional stress can have strange effects on the mind and body, so I think I should stay with them, for the afternoon at least."

"Very well, Doctor," Falken said, "if you need anything ..."

"Yes, Herbert, I do need something. I need you to give this family justice. Charles was an imperfect man, but he did not deserve this. His family most certainly does not. Give them peace. Find the murderer and send him to hell."

His spine tingling, Falken nodded and moved to the front door.

CHAPTER FIVE

A five-foot-high brick wall topped with black iron fencing enclosed the corner lot that was 2000 Tower Grove Avenue. The property was dominated by a two-story brick home with a full-front porch, side service entrance, dormer attic windows, slate roof, and a five-story observation tower rising two stories above the attic. Behind the house was a formal garden, still in the throes of development, laundry-drying area, kitchen garden, and back gate.

The Missouri Botanical Garden—commonly known as Shaw's Garden, in honor of Henry Shaw, the British-born philanthropist who built it—was directly across Tower Grove Avenue to the west; Tower Grove Park, also established by Shaw, was to the south across Magnolia Avenue.

The police department carriage lurched over a dislodged brick paver. Falken winced and gasped as his tender ribs protested. Morrissey cuffed the driver and cursed his carelessness. The carriage stopped at the corner of Magnolia and Tower Grove, and Falken and Westfall dismounted.

Morrissey joined them and walked to Falken's front gate. Confident the driver could not hear, he said to Falken. "Have your say."

"Why did you end the interview?"

"Because I didn't want his reply in Westfall's journal. There's nothing to be gained from peeking into old graves. Old, unmarked graves."

"I thought it had to be something like that."

"How can you be sure there isn't a connection?" Westfall interjected.

Morrissey looked up and down the street, inhaled the mixed fragrances wafting over from Shaw's Garden, and clasped his hands behind his back. "Because the last case was more than ten years ago."

Westfall was indignant. "How many *old, unmarked graves?*"

"Simmer down, Westfall," Falken said. "It doesn't matter."

"Like hell—"

"Westfall, calm yourself and think rationally," Falken said. "An important point has come to light." He turned to Morrissey. "Garrett had no qualms about acting decisively to counter a threat, real or perceived. Correct?"

Morrissey nodded.

Pride bruised, but in control, Westfall said, "Then why is he dead?"

"Surely you can see it. One must be in close to swing a club or stab a man." Falken faced his aide and brushed lint from the young man's collar. "As close as I am to you. Do you feel threatened or uneasy at this moment?"

"No."

"There you have it. Garrett knew his murderer."

Unconvinced, Westfall said, "What if he was attacked from behind? Or drunk?"

"He was stabbed here"—Falken ran a hand down the front of his own torso—"not in the back. Doing so to a man of Garrett's size from behind would be very unlikely." He touched his hairline. "And the blows to the head are too far forward to have been inflicted from the rear."

"Garrett liked his drink, but he never got bleary-eyed," Morrissey said. "At least not in public. Drunks are easy prey."

Westfall remained obstinate. "He could have been distracted. Tricked. Ambushed. Overwhelmed by a gang."

"While almost anything is possible in theory," Falken said, "we must accept the evidence at hand. Garrett was armed, and he was a man who tended to err on the side of caution. Experience made him wary. I'm sure he knew the pitfalls of this city like a captain knows the shoals of his homeport. No, strangers didn't do this and then simply disappear. His guard was down because he trusted his assailant. He was also experiencing financial distress, and I think this fact lies very near to the core of this case."

"Money really is the root of all evil," Morrissey said. "So, what's next?"

"Not much more can be accomplished on a Sunday. Tomorrow morning, I'll try to retrace Garrett's final hours. Depending on what I learn, that could take most of the day. So the bookkeeper will have to wait until Tuesday."

Confused, Westfall said, "You just said the financials might be the key. Why not pursue that first?"

Falken's eyes narrowed, and he pinched his chin contemplatively. "Because Garrett was also a liar. He was in the city, while his household believed he was in Illinois. I want to know why."

Westfall was even more confused. "How can you know for sure where he was?"

Falken sighed and spoke as if to a backward child. "A corpse dropped in the river on the Illinois side would hardly wash up on this side. The channel's far too wide and lacks any sharp bends. Really, Westfall, at times I think your fall from that horse disabled your mind instead of your leg."

The younger man's face reddened.

Morrissey walked away and boarded the carriage. "I'm not welcome across the river, so you're on your own there. I'll send a carriage Tuesday morning at seven." He gestured to the driver, who slapped the reins on the horse's backs and the carriage began rolling. "Be careful over there, Major. A thousand white men and ten thousand Negroes have gone across the river and never come back."

As the carriage moved away, Morrissey finished berating his driver. "Stupid pig. Keep your mind and eyes on the road. Embarrass me like that again and I'll have your balls for breakfast. I'm sure it'd be a small and wholly unsatisfying meal, but I'll have them all the same."

Falken removed his jacket and tie, and unbuttoned his collar. "I'm going to the park for some shade," he told Westfall. "Tell Owen I'll require a bath at six, and a fresh suit; this one is soaked through. Tell him to lay out the new gray jacket with burgundy vest and black trousers. Then he can have the evening off. We'll dine at Planter's on the way."

"May I infer that we're going to Mrs. Bannon's?"

"Unless you have some previously unvoiced objection. Our search takes us to East St. Louis. We'll get an earlier start in the morning if we're already there."

"No objections, Major. None at all."

CHAPTER SIX

Falken and Westfall walked out of Planter House Hotel at Fourth and Pine. Commonly called Planter's, modern functionality combined with an Old World feel made it the finest hotel in St. Louis. The building was a ten-story inverted E-shape, with a mixture of Italian and French Renaissance rococo architecture. The layout allowed natural light into all four hundred rooms. The main restaurant, heralded as the most elegant room in the city, had Doric columns and was decorated in empire green and silver. First-class fare, offered at premium prices, satisfied St. Louis residents and visitors alike.

Standing under the main entrance's cast-iron portico, Falken savored pleasantly cool, though sooty, evening air. A pall of coal smoke, temporarily washed away by the overnight rain, was returning.

Around them, the sidewalks were crowded. Men in frock coats and top hats, plain suits and bowlers, or rough working garb escorted women wearing summer dresses and hats, or bonnets, of varying design and extravagance. Late-evening strollers ran the gamut from bejeweled and polished to plain and scruffy. Children trailed behind their parents, some of whom pushed baby carriages. Wagons, carts and carriages drawn by horses, mules and men squeaked and clattered along the downtown streets.

An open-carriage St. Louis sputtered past, annoying a skittish mule. The mule stopped in the middle of the busy intersection. Falken and others watched as traffic diverted around the stalled wagon. The teamster spoke to the mule. The mule turned its head to the rear and brayed in reply. The man spoke more loudly and gestured with his free hand. The animal responded with another bray, but remained still. A shaken fist was answered with a snort. The man stood up, hands on hips, and glared, while cursing the beast for its stubbornness; he received another bray for his effort. The teamster grabbed his buggy whip and pointed it at the mule. The animal looked away, still refusing to move. Out of patience, the man cracked the whip over the mule's flank. In response, the animal backed up a few steps. Caught off balance, the man swayed forward, jerked backward, and tumbled over the seat into the empty wagon bed. With a triumphant bray and a shake of the head, the mule plodded forward.

Laughing, Falken tipped his black homburg to the mule, stepped out to the curb, and hailed a carriage-for-hire. An enclosed four-passenger carriage, pulled by a pair of bay horses, rolled to an abrupt stop. The driver stared suspiciously at Falken's battered face, still obvious in the dimming twilight, but appeared to defer to his dress, manner, and the fact that he had just come out of the finest hotel in the city.

"Where to, gentlemen?"

"East St. Louis."

"No, I don't go over there." The driver pointed east. "Darkies'll slit your throat for a quarter."

"Would you cross the bridge for double the fare?"

The driver spat. "Nothing can entice me to enter Illinoistown. And you'd be well advised to stay clear." He slapped the reins, horseshoes clopped, and the carriage creaked away.

"It's not that bad," Westfall said, "aside from the smell, hordes of blowflies, drunken brawls, and gangs of thugs."

"Everything in this world must be balanced by something else," Falken replied. "If St. Louis is the heart and soul of the Mississippi, East St. Louis is the bowel."

A hansom cab rolled up and stopped adjacent to Falken and his aide. The driver leaned over from his perch at the rear and said, "Did I hear you say you want to cross the bridge?"

"Yes," Falken said.

"Did I also hear you mention a double fare?"

"You did."

"And where would you be going?"

"Are you familiar with Mrs. Bannon's?"

With a wry grin, the driver winked and replied, "Never heard of it, sir."

"Then you're just the man we want," Falken said, and climbed into the two-passenger, one-horse, black carriage.

Westfall struggled a bit with his stiff leg and plopped down on the seat beside him.

As the hansom turned onto Washington Street and headed for the bridge, Falken became uneasy. Lips, mouth and throat went dry; his chest tightened, and an icy ball settled in his belly. He had endured these sensations before, every time he crossed the bridge, in fact. However, this time he felt something else, different yet familiar. The bridge evoked all-consuming memories and emotions, and he was not able to focus on the oddity and identify its source.

He tensed when the wheels bumped onto the bridge's upper-road deck. A train, chugging along the lower-rail deck, reverberated through the seat. He felt lightheaded and nauseous. Sweat beaded on his forehead, and dampened his underarms and palms.

Habitually, he fixated on the spot. He wanted to look away, but could not. The desire to not see magnified his guilt and shame. From toes to ears, every muscle drew taut; he dared not blink; his heart thundered; his soul ached. The cab seemed to crawl along, prolonging the anguish.

A slideshow of images flashed before his mind's eye: Anna on the bridge, laughing and smiling; her loving gaze; her lips moving, saying something; her broken body on the river bank; Garrett's corpse at the river's edge; Anna; Garrett; Anna; Garrett. *Anna!*

When the spot passed from view, Falken exhaled and went limp. He felt faint, cold, alone. For some reason he couldn't understand, it was always worse at night. If only …

"What's it like to love someone that much?" Westfall broke the silence.

"What?"

"It's been, what, fifteen years, and still you can't bear to pass by there. You must've loved her more than life itself. I've never known that kind of passion."

"'Better to have loved and lost, than never to have loved at all.' Sometimes, I wonder if it shouldn't be the other way around."

"Do you mean that?"

Falken reached inside his jacket and withdrew his cigar case. Pulling the top off, he offered one to Westfall.

The young man sighed. "Thank you, no."

Falken pulled out a long, thick, nearly black cigar, replaced the top, and took his clipper from a pocket stitched onto the case. In the dim glow of the cab's lantern, he clipped the ends, stowed the tool, and pocketed his case. He produced a box of matches from another pocket and struck one. As the small flame flared, he saw a man walking on the bridge. He realized the man could probably see them from that little bit of light. A tingle ran down his spine; he stared ahead, motionless.

"Major?" Westfall blew out the match. "What are you doing? It nearly burned your fingers."

Falken leaned forward, peering ahead. The walking man and several wagons, laden with barrels and heavy sacks, were moving in the opposite direction. He twisted on the seat and craned his neck outside the cab. At least one carriage lantern glowed behind them, intermittently silhouetting a horse and rider in between.

Westfall pulled him back onto the seat. "What are you doing?"

The feeling was there again, no longer masked by Falken's emotions. Someone is watching me, he thought. Someone, somewhere, was watching him this very minute. Tracking his movements. But who? And why?

"Major?"

"Yes, what?"

"I said, what's troubling you?"

"Nothing. I'm just thinking." Falken struck another match and lit his cigar, with a sense of … what? Fear? Foreboding? Paranoia? He drew until the tip glowed, then discarded the match.

The hansom cab stopped before a three-story brick building with a raised porch that resembled a small hotel. In fact, it had been the East Side Inn for several years until the proprietor had wagered the property deed on a heart flush and lost. The new owner was no hotelier, and had no desire to learn the trade, so he leased the premises to an acquaintance. A simple hand-painted sign, nailed to the porch railing, read:

TIPPERARY SOCIAL CLUB
• MEMBERS ONLY •

Falken paid the cab driver the agreed-upon fare, plus a modest gratuity. Then he and Westfall mounted the porch steps. Halfway to the door, he turned around, and looked up and down the street. The cab disappeared around a corner, all was dark and shadowy, and most of the district's establishments were quiet. Nothing moved, yet the feeling that he was being watched remained bothersome, like an itch he couldn't reach.

"Just thinking again?"

Falken turned back and crossed the porch.

Someone inside was playing the piano. Both men recognized the syncopated rhythm of ragtime, which had become popular in any establishment with a Negro piano player on either side of the river.

Falken rang the doorbell. "That can't be Abraham."

"You would know better than I," Westfall said, "but whoever's playing, it's quite good."

There was a metallic click as the lock was turned. The door was opened by a buxom, green-eyed brunette, clad in a yellow dress that prominently displayed her décolletage and accentuated the rest of her femininity. Her neutral expression brightened, then furrowed with concern.

"My word," she said to Falken, "you're a sight. Does it hurt as bad as it looks?"

Falken felt his face color and heard Westfall snicker. "Good evening, Jane. Nothing to worry about; it looks much worse than it is."

"Jade, sir. Mrs. Bannon says I'm to call myself Jade," the brunette said, as she stepped aside.

With a last glance at the street, Falken crossed the threshold. "Of course, how silly of me. Good evening, Jade."

"And a good evening to you, Mr. Smith." As Westfall stepped into the foyer, she added, "And to you as well, Mr. Smith."

"You're new here?" said Westfall, as the music stopped.

"Yes, sir. Came out from Boston at the beginning of the summer." Jade closed and locked the door. "Please step into the parlor, gentlemen. I'll let Mrs. Bannon know you're here." She paused, looked at Falken and added, "I truly hope it doesn't hurt much, but it certainly looks like it does."

Westfall watched her hips sway down the dimly lit hallway until she disappeared into shadow beyond the main staircase.

Falken slid the pocket doors open and walked into the bright smoky parlor, with Westfall in tow. Several well-heeled gentlemen and a dozen provocatively-dressed, attractive, young women glanced at them. While discreet nods were exchanged with a few of the men, open-mouthed women stared at Falken's swollen black eye; a tall dark blonde shook her head with a knowing, resigned expression.

Membership in the Tipperary Social Club was by invitation only. An established member could extend said invitation, but the proprietress, Mrs. Bannon, retained the right to approve or reject anyone. Though some had tried, no one was permitted to buy or bully his way onto the membership roster, nor were memberships handed out as political gifts. She catered to wealthy discriminating clients, mostly St. Louisans, who valued discretion and quality above all else. Several had heard her say, "Any reasonably intelligent woman can run a stable of two-dollar whores. But it takes a real madam to manage a high-class brothel."

A Negro Falken had never seen sat at the piano, sipping from a tumbler dark with bourbon. He put down the tumbler and announced, "This next piece is something new I've been working on. I call it 'Maple Leaf Rag.'"

As he began playing, a slim, auburn-haired beauty about Falken's age glided into the room and closed the pocket doors. Gentlemen rose and bowed to their hostess. With a flash of smile, she waved them back to their chairs and glanced around the room. Her conservatively-cut burgundy dress outlined the smallest, though still ample, bosom in the room. Apparently satisfied all was in order, she went to Falken's side.

"Jesus, you look like hell," she whispered with an Irish lilt that belied her fiery personality.

Tapping his foot with the tune, Falken replied, "Hello to you, too."

"I mean it. Your eye looks awful." Sarah. Bannon brushed ash from his sleeve. "And I hope it hurts like the devil."

Falken winked with his good eye and asked, "Who's he?" as the piano continued to sing.

"A friend of Abraham's. Hoblin. Goblin. No, Joplin. Yes, that's it, Scott Joplin. Abraham asked if he could come in and play tonight." She turned to Westfall. "Good evening, James."

Westfall nodded toward the piano. "He's quite good. Perhaps you should hire him."

"I've already tried. He's a piano teacher and composer, he says. Told me he's just visiting from Sedalia. Business in the city with a music publisher or some such thing."

"Maybe he can give Abraham a few lessons while he's here," Falken said.

She ignored the remark and continued speaking to Westfall. "It's been a while. Would you care to sit with Desiree?"

Westfall glanced around. "Well, actually I'd like to meet Jade, if she's available."

Mrs. Bannon smiled. "You'll like her. A tad gabby, but otherwise exquisite." She signaled a freckled redhead and the tall dark blonde.

The young women crossed the parlor, smiling brightly. "Yes, ma'am?" they said in unison.

To the redhead, Mrs. Bannon said, "Ask Jade to come in here and take her place at the door."

After a flash of disappointment and perhaps jealousy, the redhead nodded and left.

As the tune ended and everyone applauded, Jade closed the pocket doors and approached her employer. "Yes, ma'am?"

"Jade, I'd like you to meet a dear friend, Mr. Smith."

The brunette beamed, accepted Westfall's arm, and guided him to a quiet corner at the back of the room.

To the dark blonde, Mrs. Bannon said, "I'm not to be disturbed unless the house is on fire or someone is dying." Then she took Falken's hand and led him to the doors.

CHAPTER SEVEN

Anna!

Falken jerked awake, grasping at the darkness, lungs heaving.

Sarah stirred and sat up, the bedsheet spilling off of her naked breasts. She reached out and touched his back. "Darling, you're drenched and trembling."

She got out of bed, went to the washbasin and returned with a large towel. Drying his skin and damp hair, she said, Nightmare?"

"Yes, sorry I woke you."

"Which one?"

Falken shivered involuntarily then sank back onto the pillow. "The bridge."

Sarah pulled the sheet up, rested her head on his shoulder, and draped her left arm over his chest. Her fingers traced a long jagged scar running from his right collarbone to his armpit. "Tell me."

"It doesn't matter."

Rising onto her elbow, Sarah slapped his chest. "Goddamn you, Herbert, it matters to me." Her tone softened. "I want to help, to take away your pain, but I can't do that if you won't talk to me. Tell me what happened."

He remained silent.

"Herbert Falken, you share my bed and practically bounce me out of it at all hours of the night with these damned nightmares. At least you can explain why we never get a full night's sleep together."

"Very well." He rubbed his eyes as she settled back into place. "Her name was Anna, Anna Schrader."

"How old was she?"

"Nineteen. I'd returned from West Point, a fledgling second lieutenant, and we were to be married. Two days before the wedding, on a lark, Anna wanted to walk out on the bridge and watch the steamboats. We'd booked a cabin aboard *City of St. Louis* and planned to honeymoon in New Orleans. She was fascinated by the prospect of riding a floating palace down the river and back. As we started across, she was like a child, speaking animatedly, fantasizing about the trip. She kept asking question after question. She wanted to know about the boilers, sidewheels, electrical generators, even the plumbing, of all things."

Falken shivered again, and his voice croaked. "We were walking near the edge of the bridge to avoid the wagons. She took my hand and began pulling me so I'd walk faster. I resisted her tug, playfully. She began jerking my arm to try and pull me off balance … Her hand slipped from mine. She laughed. She reeled backward, laughing, arms flailing for balance. I laughed with her. The look on her face was pure joy. Then … she collided with the railing. Her eyes went wide, her lips moved without sound. She … tumbled over the side. I ran forward, leaned over the rail …"

He swallowed hard. "The police assured me she died instantly. After her funeral, I boarded a train to Fort Riley."

Sarah's tears dripped onto his chest. "Is that what you see in the dream?"

"In the dream it's after the fall. I'm standing in the center of the bridge, looking at the river. Anna stands in the river, unmoved by the current. She's wearing a flowing silk gown, and a bright aura outlines her form. She asks, 'Why did you let me fall? Why didn't you save me?' Then she crumbles into a cloud of dust, saying, 'You did this.'"

"Darling, you didn't do anything," Sarah said. "It was happenstance. Terrible unfortunate happenstance, and you weren't to blame."

"I wish I could believe that."

"You must believe it, because it's the truth." Sarah kissed his chest and neck, as her tears dried up. "You're a good man, Herbert Falken, a good, decent, courageous, brilliant man. Try to remember that." Then she kissed him passionately and rolled over on top of him.

With the sun fully up, Falken roused himself from Sarah's bed. He used the chamber pot and went to the washbasin to make himself presentable.

Sarah had risen a few minutes earlier, donned a silk dressing gown and gone downstairs, leaving the door slightly ajar. Lathering his face with a shaving brush he kept there, Falken heard movement and voices in the corridor. He thought it sounded like Jane—correction, Jade— and Sylvia, the tall dark blonde.

"Why am I up early to cook breakfast for a john? He had me up half the night."

"You don't look like it was a torturous night."

"He knows his way around a woman's body, but still."

"We're up early because Mr. James is not a john."

"What do you mean?"

"He works for the major and comes here as the major's guest. That makes him special."

"Special how?"

"Well, he and the major are to be welcomed in and shown every hospitality, any time of day or night. Refuse them an accommodation and you'll be out in the street before the next hour chimes. They're also among the few with overnight privileges. But unlike the others, in the morning they get breakfast cooked and served by Sarah and us. And they're never charged."

"No money? She didn't tell—"

"Don't get your bloomers in a bunch. Sarah will pay you for last night out of her own pocket."

"Why?"

"Don't be stupid, girl. The way she looks at him, the special rules that only apply to him … she's in love."

"In love? With a john? That's rich. Next you're going to tell me she's faithful to him." After a brief pause, she said, "Noooo."

"Keep your voice down. It's true. Since the major started coming here, Sarah quit taking johns for herself. She had a string of regulars who'd shell out five dollars a lay, and she passed them off to me. Now, not a word …"

The voices faded as the women descended the staircase.

Falken stared at his reflection in the mirror. *And here I was assuming it was gratitude,* he thought, *or a simple need for companionship. Whore or not, she was a fine woman, and he enjoyed her company. But love? Damn.*

He shaved quickly, cutting himself twice. Then he dressed.

He did not love her in return. There was no denying it. He wasn't sure he could ever love a woman again. *Damn.*

He looked at Sarah's bed, wardrobe, vanity, and the trunk where she stored her keepsakes. Her scent was still in the air; her passionate moaning gasps rang in his ears; he felt her hands on him and his on her; he could still feel her moving against him. This room was one of the few sources of joy in his life.

Falken opened the door and stepped out of Sarah's room, wondering if he would ever see it again.

CHAPTER EIGHT

Falken and Westfall exited the Tipperary and descended the porch steps to the street. Falken thought that Westfall's leg seemed to function more normally this morning, his cane serving as more of an accessory than a requirement.

Westfall stood on the sidewalk with the red-leather satchel gripped in his left hand. "What is it, Major? You hardly touched your food."

Falken showed his aide-de-camp a tight neutral expression. "Nothing."

"I'm tired of being told nothing's wrong when something obviously is. I can't assist you properly if I'm perpetually kept in the dark."

Falken stroked his handlebar mustache. "This sounds pathetically cliché, but you cannot possibly comprehend my position so there's no point explaining it."

"You're right, it is a pathetic attempt to dodge my question." Westfall looked back at the brothel. He thought for a moment, then his eyes lit with perception. "You didn't say ten words at the table, and Sarah's smiling eyes became forlorn. You had a row.

She thought all was forgiven, but you disagree. And now you're both in a foul, dark mood."

"Well, you got one part right," Falken said, raising his arm and waving.

A hansom pulled over to the curb and stopped. The cab was faded and worn, but the axle didn't squeak, the wheels were sound, and the horse looked healthy and strong. "Where to, gentlemen?" the driver said.

"Garrett Stable, for a start," Falken said. "We'll need to crisscross town on our business."

"That can be expensive, sir."

Falken reached into his pocket, then flipped the driver a Morgan dollar, followed by another. "Is that sufficient retainer?"

"It'll do for now," the driver replied with a toothy grin. "Please watch your step and climb aboard."

Falken glanced up at Sarah's second-floor window, shook his head, and boarded the cab with a hollow stomach.

When Westfall was seated the Friesian horse pulled away easily, then settled into a gentle trot.

Leaving the red-light district's daytime inactivity, they began seeing people and animals moving in every direction. Women carried crude burlap handbags bearing the morning's market purchases, some with children in tow. Men pushed or pulled carts, hawking services from blade sharpening to tinkering. Other cart merchants sold fruits, vegetables, and cured meats to those unable or unwilling to walk to the markets. Large wagons drawn by teams of draft horses were laden high with stacks of barrels. Smaller wagons pulled by horses or mules hauled crates, burlap sacks, and loose cargo. Merchants and trusted clerks strode from one appointment to the next, and carriages conveyed passengers. Mounted policemen kept a watchful eye over everything.

Small knots of mostly younger men, and a few boys, stood idle here and there, watching and waiting. They were readily marked as thugs and petty criminals. No one else could afford to loiter so casually on a workday and still earn a living. Even the destitute scurried about asking for odd jobs, or actively seeking an opportunity to scavenge a small meal.

Chimneys billowed black smoke; steam hissed from corroded piping; engines chugged; trains clattered; animals snorted, brayed and barked; flies buzzed; and foul odors mingled with the scent of baking bread and cooking meat.

It was just another Monday morning in a purpose-built industrial city.

Falken and Westfall stepped down in front of the Garrett Cartage Breeding Stable.

"We shouldn't be long," Falken told the driver.

The cab driver spat a thick stream of tobacco juice. "Take your time, sir. I'm at your service."

A wagonload of soiled straw, steaming in the morning air, rolled past. Investigator and aide walked to the stable office and went inside.

A paunchy, balding clerk behind a small desk peered over his spectacles as they approached. "Help you, sir?" he said to Falken.

"Herbert Falken. I wish to speak with Mr. Vesper."

A short, thick man with the forearms and biceps of a laborer looked up from behind a larger desk. "I'm Vesper."

Falken approached and handed over his card. "Is there someplace we could have a quiet word?"

Vesper examined the card and said to the clerk, "Go get some air."

The clerk stood, huffed and stomped out the door.

"How can I help you?" Vesper indicated a pair of soiled chairs.

With all the grace he could muster, Westfall pulled out his handkerchief, placed it on a chair, sat and prepared to take notes.

Falken remained standing. "Are you aware of what's happened to Mr. Garrett?"

Vesper responded with a quizzical look. "No, what?"

Falken explained briefly and gave the manager some time to absorb the unfortunate news. Then he said, "I understand Garrett met with you Saturday."

Vesper eyed Westfall's journal and pen suspiciously, and shook his head. "I don't know how you came by that, but you're mistaken. The last time I spoke with Mr. Garrett was a week, no, ten days ago. And I went to Garrett House. He rarely came over here."

"Was a meeting for Saturday canceled?"

"No, there wasn't any meeting. I was here most of the day tending to a sick colt. If Mr. Garrett had been on the property, I'd have known."

Falken stroked his mustache. "Are you familiar with Garrett's other concerns on this side of the river?"

"Vaguely. All the managers, here and in the city, attend a monthly meeting at the House. I listen to their reports and hear his instructions to the others."

"What I mean is, when you say Garret rarely came over here, did you mean the stable specifically, or East St. Louis in general? Was he in the habit of visiting his other subsidiaries?"

"No, Mr. Garrett preferred to stay in the city. I've been here twenty-four years and I've seen him on this side maybe five times. He sent for people if he needed to discuss business in person."

"Have there been any financial difficulties? Late payroll? Accounts payable outstanding?"

"You think that has something to do with … with what happened?"

"How serious is the problem?"

"I'm not sure I should be discussing this with you."

Falken leaned forward, resting his hands on Vesper's desk. "In matters like this, *everything* is potentially important. One piece of information leads to another, and another, and so on. I cannot identify the important pieces unless I see everything."

Vesper scratched his head. "I've had to let two-thirds of my men go. My feed vendor is cutting us off, unless this pile of invoices," he said, pointing to a stack of papers, "is paid in full."

"When did Garrett stop paying his bills?"

"The invoice on the bottom is from April."

"Did he have a plan to become solvent again?"

"If he did, he didn't share it with me or the others. I've talked to Morgan, Unger and some others. We're all on the cliff's edge waiting to be rescued or knocked off."

Falken nodded to Westfall, who repacked the satchel. At the door, Falken turned back and said, "One last question. Can you think of anyone who would want to harm Garrett?"

"You mean other than the men who've lost their jobs and those he owed money?"

The Friesian horse clopped along a freshly swept business district street in Belleville, Illinois. Located fifteen miles south-southeast of East St. Louis, the small town served as the St. Clair county seat. It was also home to the upper middle-class merchants, bankers and landholders who quietly prospered just beyond the big city's shadow. From the town's fringes, a patchwork of farms, large and small, stretched to the horizon and beyond.

As he suspected, Falken's interviews with Morgan and Unger had verified Vesper's claims, without adding anything of significance. Garrett had been teetering on the verge of bankruptcy, but his managers did not know why, and nor did any of the three men meet with him on Saturday.

The cab driver pulled to the curb and stopped in front of a two-story brick building with an ornate bronze parapet. It was nearly identical to every other building on the block. A sign above the entrance read:

DECKER STEAMBOAT LINE
ST. LOUIS, MEMPHIS & NEW ORLEANS
EST. 1845

Falken and Westfall dismounted and walked inside.

"How can I help you, gentlemen?" said a leather-faced white-haired man with bushy muttonchops. He wore a white shirt, navy-blue vest with matching bowtie, and black trousers. A briar pipe hung from the corner of his mouth.

"Mr. Decker?" Falken replied.

"Yes. You are?"

Falken introduced himself and Westfall, and handed over his card.

"*Major* Falken, I presume?"

"Yes, sir."

"You're inquiring about Charles?"

Falken nodded. "You know what happened?"

"I expect everyone knows." Decker held up a newspaper. The front-page headline read:

ST. LOUIS ALDERMAN GARRETT
MURDERED!

"Please, come back to my office," Decker said.

Leaning heavily on a cane, he made his way around the long counter and led them down a short corridor. He opened the only door on the right and waved them in. The spacious private office was furnished with a massive oak desk, matching credenza, and several armchairs arranged in a sitting area. The walls were decorated with paintings of a couple dozen sidewheelers and a handful of old sternwheelers. A large portrait—obviously a younger Decker in the uniform of a naval lieutenant—hung behind his desk.

Decker guided them to the sitting area, indicated chairs, and seated himself opposite.

Falken nodded at the portrait. "River monitors?"

"No, the navy leased our fleet to transport troops and supplies." Decker pointed with his pipe at the painting to the right of his portrait. "I commanded *Grafton*. It was a different time, simple, unambiguous. We all understood what we were doing and why."

"I'm attempting to retrace Garrett's actions. Did he call on you this past Saturday?"

Decker pursed his lips and made eye contact. "Charles did not, as you say, call on me. I demanded he come here to explain himself."

Falken, expecting another blank wall, was momentarily taken aback. "So Garrett was here?"

"I've told you he was. And I presumed you already knew that, as you're here asking questions."

"What time did he arrive?"

"Just before the noon hour. We had a light luncheon, then came back here."

"So you did not receive him at your home?"

"No, we didn't socialize. Our relationship was strictly business, and I've come to regret that."

Falken's confusion grew with every answer. "Perhaps it would be best if you recount the details of the meeting and your reasons for demanding it."

"River commerce is waning, has been for a number of years. Everyone's shipping by rail these days. Just fifteen years ago, we had a fleet of seventeen boats. Today, seven remain afloat. But there are enough loyal clients to keep what remains profitable.

"Mid-May, I received a lengthy letter from Henry DuBois of DuBois Trading House, New Orleans. Our fathers started doing business during the Mexican War. The gist of Henry's letter was he intended to sever our relationship forthwith because I was treating him so poorly. He accused me of leaving his cargo on the wharf and insulting him with feeble excuses.

"Utterly confused and just a bit perturbed, I boarded the first southbound boat and met with Henry to have it out. I was of a mind to thrash him for slandering my name and the reputation of this line. But before matters got out of hand he showed me five letters on our letter paper bearing what appeared to be my signature. Each was a contrived apology for failing to service contracted cargo, with an assurance it wouldn't happen again. My signature at the bottom of each was a forgery.

"Three of our boats were in New Orleans at the time. I called on the captains and discovered the truth. Charles had replaced our cargo agents—that is, *my* cargo agents—at our port offices with his own men. The new agents were placing un-manifested cargo aboard the boats. To make room, legitimate shipments were left behind."

Falken interrupted. "A smuggling operation?"

"Yes. Under threat of prosecution, all three captains detailed the particulars and confessed their own culpability. I discharged them and the agent. Then I dispatched telegrams to Memphis and St. Louis ordering the dismissal of everyone involved. When I came home, I summoned Charles. He invented one excuse after another to cancel appointments. I went to Garrett House for a confrontation, but he evaded me at every turn. Finally, he acquiesced when I threatened to take the matter up with the U.S. Attorney. Of course, the meeting was futile. He sat in this office and denied everything. Even went so far as to suggest I was senile and had imagined the whole affair. After he left, I went to my attorney and instructed him to do whatever was necessary to dissolve our partnership."

"There's a third partner, a Mr. Fulton of Memphis?"

"Yes, he's a silent partner. Legally, he owns our warehouses and port offices, but he isn't involved in running the line."

"How did this partnership evolve?"

"The panic of ninety-three. One of the banks I was using at the time failed, leaving me cash poor. Investors were scared, so I brokered the best deal available. Fulton bought the port facilities, and Garrett got half of the fleet. I retained my positions as company president and commodore, but Garrett and I shared executive authority."

"What was he smuggling?"

"I haven't been able to find out."

"When did he leave?"

"About half past two."

"What happens to Garrett's share?"

"It's non-transferable. Fulton and I can divide it equally, or I can purchase his portion. I haven't contacted him yet."

Falken crossed his legs and stroked his mustache. "Mr. Decker, you do realize that circumstances make you a prime suspect. Garrett's death saves you a considerable sum in legal fees, and obviates the need to buy back his entire holding. It also spares you the embarrassment of airing dirty linen in public."

The aged river captain filled his pipe while projecting an air of fearlessness. "I suppose that's one way of looking at it."

"Where were you from suppertime Saturday until yesterday morning?"

"At home, alone. My wife passed last year"—Decker crossed himself—"bless her soul, and nearly all my friends are gone. Yesterday morning I attended mass at St Luke." He struck a match and lit his pipe.

"You have no one to vouch for your whereabouts?"

Decker shook his head and exhaled smoke. "My housekeeper has weekends off. No one has time for an old man."

"Who received the illicit cargo?"

"That too remains a mystery. The captains told me the shipments went into our St. Louis warehouse. From there I've learned that Garrett wagons hauled it away to unknown destinations. Sometimes it was hogsheads or nail kegs, other times flour sacks or steamer trunks."

Falken stood. "I may need to speak with you again. Thank you for your time."

Decker rose, with the aid of his cane, and escorted them out.

In the outer office, Falken said, "There is another point I need to clarify. You say you didn't socialize with Garrett."

Decker nodded.

"So he's never been an overnight guest in your home."

Decker's eyes narrowed, and he pointed his pipe at Falken. "If that son of a bitch had ever crossed my threshold I would have burned the house to the ground."

CHAPTER NINE

The late afternoon sun scorched the city through a cloudless sky. Falken and Westfall stepped off the trolley and trudged homeward. They bore the look and odor of men who had been on the road all day: dust soiled their faces and clothing; large dark stains showed under their arms and down their backs; dry lips and scratchy voices told of unquenched thirst; squinting eyes and drawn expressions bespoke fatigue.

Nonetheless, the young aide managed a burst of enthusiasm once they were out of earshot of the cab driver, or anyone else. "Do you really think Decker did it?"

"Certainly not with his own hand. Walking across the room is a challenge for him. But he could have hired it done."

"Precisely what I'm thinking. He has a strong enough motive."

"True, but murder is a three-legged stool. In addition to means and motive, one must also have opportunity."

Westfall's face screwed up in thought for several moments. Then he said, "A frail old man couldn't have ridden here and back. But he could've sent a telegram or dispatched a messenger."

Falken glanced sideways at his aide-de-camp. "Oh sure, Decker strolls into Western Union, writes out a murder order, hands it to the clerk and says, 'Send this right away, then forget all about it.'" He shook his head, regretting his sarcasm. Extreme heat or cold tended to make him surly, and checking his foul mood required conscious effort. "A messenger is doubtful for the same reason."

"Then how?"

"If it was Decker, he would have had the mechanism in place already. After the meeting, a simple prearranged signal, such as an innocuous telegram, could have triggered the action."

They crossed Tower Grove Avenue as a pair of buggies raced along Magnolia; to their astonishment, a sneering, cussing woman was driving the lead buggy.

Westfall opened the arched iron gate and an electric switch closed, activating three buzzers in the house: in the kitchen, cellar, and attic hallway.

Owen opened the front door as they mounted the porch steps. "Good afternoon, Major."

"I don't know how good it is, but thank you, Owen."

"Your mail's in the library, sir. A policeman delivered a letter as well."

Falken stepped into his home and sighed with relief. There was no other feeling like returning home. "That can wait for now. I need a cool drink, a bath and fresh clothing, in that order."

Westfall closed the door as Mrs. Howard entered the hallway from the kitchen. She was a short, plump, dark-skinned woman with an enormous bosom. Her black hair, streaked with gray, was held back with a pale blue sweat-stained bandana that matched her apron. She clucked and shook her head.

"One day they're going to carry you out of that place, Major," she said. "Then where'll you be?"

Falken accepted his housekeeper's rebuke in silence. She cared for him like a son.

Mrs. Howard thrust her chin at Westfall. "And you're supposed to be looking after him. Why did you let him go down to the levee and get whupped on like that?"

Westfall blushed and looked at the floor.

Owen, standing silently to one side, failed to suppress a grin.

Mrs. Howard turned on Owen. "And don't you stand there grinning like the cat that got the cream. When I'm not around, it's your job to take care of both of them. Sweet Jesus, save me from men's foolish pride."

"Mrs. Howard, I am foolish and thirsty," Falken said. "I would be eternally grateful for a pitcher of your iced tea."

"Uh-huh." She shook a fat finger at him. "You be grateful I don't black the other eye and send you to bed without your supper." She turned away, muttering to herself.

Owen relieved Westfall of the satchel, went down the hallway and turned left into the library.

Falken turned left into the parlor. Brown-leather club chairs were arranged in a horseshoe, atop a plush red-and-brown rug, in the back half of the room. Opposite the door, his father's Medal of Honor and framed citation for valor were displayed on the mantel. A photograph of President McKinley hung above. The interior walls were decorated with large paintings depicting the Battle of Bunker's Hill, the bombardment of Fort McHenry, and the Hornet's Nest at Shiloh.

Falken dropped into his chair at the head of the horseshoe beneath portraits of Generals Washington and Grant. He took a cigar from a humidor atop a small table to his left.

Westfall hobbled in with the mail and sat to Falken's right. "Nothing of significance other than this." He extended a buff envelope.

Cigar lit, Falken took the envelope and examined it. It was addressed to him, but it did not identify the sender. "This could have waited," he said. Then he pulled a penknife from his pocket and slit the envelope.

He extracted two pages; the first was a handwritten note on police department letter paper:

Major,

Included is a copy of Dr. Evans's postmortem exam report. I thought you might want to read it.

The carriage will pick you up tomorrow morning at seven. I'll be interested to hear what you learned in Illinois.

Morrissey

Falken drew on his cigar and began reading the dry, matter-of-fact report. Owen came in carrying a silver tray with two glasses and a glass pitcher of iced tea. He paused in his reading when Owen handed him a glass. After several greedy gulps, he extended the glass for a refill.

Westfall smacked his lips. "Nectar of the gods. We should bottle this and sell it."

Falken drank down another half-glass. "No one's going to buy tea in a bottle when they can easily make their own. We'd be old and gray before we made our first sale."

Falken stroked his mustache and concentrated on reading the report. When he had digested every word he handed the page to Westfall. He stroked his mustache.

When Westfall finished reading he said, "Not much there we can use."

Falken exhaled a cloud of smoke. "On the contrary, the devil is in the details. The wood splinters in Garrett's scalp are identified as ash."

"How is that important?"

"What is commonly made from ash and could be readily used to strike a man in the head?"

Westfall closed his eyes in thought. After several seconds, his eyes popped open. "A baseball bat?"

"Precisely. The report also indicates the stab wounds were made by a skinning knife."

"So we're looking for a butcher, fisherman, trapper, hunter, or a man who works in a slaughterhouse or fish market and also plays baseball. That certainly narrows the field of suspects."

Owen reentered the parlor. "Major, your bath is drawn."

"Excellent." Falken stubbed out his cigar and rose. "One piece at a time, Westfall. We shall solve this case by uncovering one piece at a time."

CHAPTER TEN

The police carriage pulled to the curb in front of Garrett House, a fairly modern six-story brick building. A trolley clattered down the middle of Market Street. Two blocks away, Tuesday morning travelers streamed in and out of Union Station's massive limestone headhouse; a steam whistle, from the train shed, heralded a departure. Wagons and carriages rolled along on both sides of the trolley line, and drivers and passengers alike stared at Falken and company as they dismounted and entered the building.

A bespectacled, clean-shaven young man stood behind a desk. "How may I help you, gentlemen?" he said.

"We need to see Mr. Garrett's bookkeeper, Mr. Keller," Captain Morrissey replied.

The clerk motioned over another young man and whispered to him.

"Please follow me, gentlemen," the young man said.

They walked down a wide oak-parquet corridor to an elevator. The maroon-jacketed operator ushered them in, closed the iron accordion gate, and pulled the control lever. The car lurched upward, which Falken noted was smoother than most. He did not like elevators. The sensation of the floor rising under him was unnatural.

After exiting the elevator on the third floor, the young man led them to a small office. He waved them through the open door.

A slight, brown-haired man, struggling to write with a bandaged right hand, looked up. His neatly organized desk took up most of the room; the office was more like a large wardrobe than an office. Obviously taken aback, he stood up straight, as if snapping to attention.

"How may I help you?" Franz Keller said with a slight German accent. He came around his desk and retrieved his jacket from a peg by the door.

While Westfall readied himself, Morrissey handled the introductions.

Jacket on, Keller said, "I apologize. This office is not large enough for visitor chairs." He moved back behind his desk and added, "What is this about?"

Falken took his cue. "You're aware of what happened to Mr. Garrett?"

Keller looked down and nodded.

"We have some questions about his finances."

Eyes still downcast, Keller replied, "I don't know if it's appropriate for me to discuss these matters with you."

Morrissey leaned forward. "If it'll assuage your ethics, we can have this conversation in *my* office."

Keller raised his eyes, and glanced from Morrissey to Falken. "I'll be as helpful as I can."

"Is it true that Garrett was on the verge of bankruptcy?" Falken said.

"He was penniless. This company is insolvent. No one here knew but me. Herr Garrett made me swear an oath to keep silent. Yesterday afternoon Herr Thornton, the vice president, came in. After I told him the truth, he left and hasn't returned." Keller pointed to the ceiling. "Most of the sixth floor either didn't come in this morning or are leaving now."

"Penniless?" Falken said. "How can that be? He owned considerable assets."

"Everything is mortgaged, buildings, inventory, land, his home, everything. That's how he kept operating the past few months. Herr Garrett's estate is worthless."

"How did that happen?"

Keller looked down again, crossed his arms and shifted from one foot to the other.

"Ethics troubling you again?" interjected Morrissey.

"No, but it's a difficult thing to say." After a moment, Keller continued. "Herr Garrett was a gambler. There's a place near Planter's. I don't know the address but he went there to play poker." He shook his head slowly. "Last January he came to me and said he'd lost fifty thousand dollars."

Westfall whistled. "That's more than most men will see in a lifetime."

Keller continued. "He needed to raise capital to pay the debt. Winter is a bad time. Men don't go out to drink our beer, and wagons and boats don't haul much. He didn't have the money. The next day he told me a man had bought his debt. He said this man would accept services … ah, favors, in lieu of cash. At first it was wagonloads of beer no one paid for. Later the wagons were used for other things without payment, then the boats. Overhead was being paid out, but very little revenue was coming in."

"Yes, we know about the smuggling," Falken said. "Who was blackmailing Garrett?"

Keller's eyes lit up. "A very dangerous man. He threatened Herr Garrett's family, threatened to do things to his daughters."

"You need not worry," Falken said. "We know how to handle dangerous men."

"His name is Devlin. Liam Devlin."

"Have you seen this Devlin?"

"Yes, he came here many times."

"Describe him."

Keller pointed at Westfall. "About his height, but thin, with short red hair, a full beard, and a jagged scar here." He touched his right cheek. "And he's missing the right ring finger."

"Do you know what Garrett's plans were for Saturday?" Falken asked.

"I kept Herr Garrett's books, not his calendar. The butler would probably know."

"Will anything be left for the widow and children?"

"Before the first snow flies, they'll be on the street with nothing but the clothes on their backs. Most creditors have either begun litigation or threatened to do so." Keller waved his hand at the pile of paper on the corner of his desk. "They're all unpaid invoices."

"Do you know where Devlin can be found?"

"No."

Falken nodded to Morrissey. "Captain, do you have any questions?"

"No, I think we're done here."

Falken withdrew a card from his wallet and handed it to Keller. "Please write your address on here. We may need to call on you again." Watching the bookkeeper struggle with his ink pen, he said, "What happened to your hand?"

"Broken beer bottle." Keller looked up sheepishly. "Budweiser. I suppose it's my punishment for being disloyal." He handed back the card.

"Thank you, Mr. Keller."

⧖

On the sidewalk, Morrissey looked up and down the street and said, "Thought that scum moved on a while ago."

"You know this Devlin?" Falken asked.

"Oh yes, I know Liam Devlin. Gives every decent Irishman a bad name. Started lying, stealing and pimping five seconds after he got off the boat. He'd sell his mother for a nickel. I thought he left the city after the last drubbing I gave him."

"Do you know anything about this gambling house near Planter's?"

Instead of answering, Morrissey said, "I have an idea." He walked a few yards up the street in the direction of Union Station and stopped at a call box.

"Does it make sense for this Devlin to kill Garrett?" Westfall asked Falken.

"You heard Keller. He was bled dry. When a cow no longer gives milk, it goes to the slaughterhouse."

Westfall nodded. "And perhaps 'three can keep a secret, if two are dead.'"

"Quoting *Poor Richard's*? I had no idea you were such a classical fellow."

Morrissey walked back and said, "I was right. The game's run out of Gordon's Hotel, down the street from Planter's. Devlin's a silent partner and uses the place for some of his enterprises."

"So the game was crooked and Garrett was targeted," Falken replied.

"It's a good bet." Morrissey chuckled at his own pun. "The merchant game, as they call it, is one of Devlin's favorite and most profitable confidence tricks. My men will be assembled in half an hour, then we're going on a raid."

Falken and Westfall watched from the far side of Pine Street as three carriages full of policemen rumbled up the street, horseshoes pounding.

Two gangsters, loitering on the street as lookouts, ran to the entrance of Gordon's Hotel. One tripped and fell hard. Four policemen sprang from the alleyways on both sides of the hotel. Two pairs of strong arms latched onto the fallen man and dragged him away. The other gangster had reached the limestone steps, but a young policeman lunged and tackled him. Another patrolman rushed up, and a flurry of punches and kicks were exchanged. The gangster howled in pain and was dragged away by his ankles, face scraping the sidewalk; the younger policeman's head was bleeding.

Three carriages stopped abruptly in front of the hotel; the horses protested at being reined in forcefully. Morrissey was in the lead carriage. Twelve uniformed men leapt from the other two carriages and charged up the steps, billy clubs in hand. The drivers dismounted and cordoned off the sidewalk and entrance.

Traffic on Pine Street stopped in both directions, and pedestrians gathered in small knots to watch the spectacle. Teamsters pointed and shouted remarks. A top-hatted gentleman with Burnside mustache and sideburns leaned out of his carriage and cheered the police. A middle-class matron with a disgusted expression shook her head.

From within the hotel, excited feminine shouts, angry masculine exclamations, slamming doors and crashing furniture could be heard.

A diminutive man dived out a second-floor side window onto the fire escape. He released the retracted iron ladder, which hit the pavement with a loud clang. One of the patrolmen below moved to the bottom of the ladder as the gangster started climbing down; another uniform appeared at the window.

Realizing he was trapped, the scrawny criminal yelled, "Come and get me!"

A teamster called out from the street, "You'll wish they hadn't, Paddy." Several other drivers laughed in response.

The sounds from within the hotel diminished, and Morrissey appeared on the steps. Surveying the scene, he pointed at his men. "Clear this street. This isn't a circus sideshow."

While the patrolmen pointed, waved their arms and barked commands, Falken and Westfall weaved through the crowd across Pine Street and ascended the hotel steps.

Morrissey huffed and said, "Devlin's not here. We bagged a handful of his men and a dozen whores." He removed his helmet and wiped his brow. "You up for a little playacting?"

Falken nodded, and Morrissey explained his plan.

Falken and Westfall stood in the dingy second-floor corridor, listening and waiting. The door of an interior room was slightly ajar.

"Talk, you Belfast scum."

Wet smacks of flesh slapping flesh were accompanied by grunts of pain.

"You're gonna talk to me or I'll send you home in a pine box."

Several dull thuds—punches to the midsection, Falken guessed— were followed by a gasping, guttural rasp.

"What's the use? This one's not smart enough to save himself."

"Say, what if we break his kneecaps? Would you like that, Paddy?"

On cue, Falken slammed the door open and marched in. "What the devil's going on here?"

Morrissey and three policemen, custodian helmets and tunics removed, snapped to attention. One barrel-chested officer had his billy club cocked and ready to swing like a bat; the other two held the bleeding, wide-eyed, diminutive gangster with his arms twisted behind his back.

"Interrogating the prisoner, Major," Morrissey said.

"Interrogating? Looks more like medieval torture to me, Captain." Falken pointed to the gangster. "Unhand that man."

The patrolmen complied, and the gangster sagged against the wall with a sigh.

Falken turned to Westfall. "Lieutenant, get these barbarians out of here and wait for my orders." He looked at Morrissey. "Captain, you and your men can expect to face charges. I will not tolerate this."

Expressions sullen, Morrissey and his men collected their things and left the room. His mouth a grim line of righteous disdain, Westfall closed the door behind them.

Falken gestured to the unmade bed. "Please have a seat, Mr. ..."

The runt of an Irishman shuffled over and sat on the foot of the bed, toes barely touching the floor. His facade of bravado had been shattered. His shoulders trembled, and his eyes welled with tears. "O'Toole."

"Do you want me to call a doctor, Mr. O'Toole?"

The gangster shook his head in reply and wiped his cheeks.

"Very well, would you care for a cigar?"

"Yes, thank you."

Falken pulled out his cigar case, removed the top, and extended it to O'Toole. The man took one, bit off the end and extended it to Falken's match. Falken then prepared and lit his own.

"I'm going to ask you some questions," Falken said. "Answer truthfully and no harm will come to you."

Eyes still scared, O'Toole nodded quickly.

"How did you choose Alderman Garrett for the merchant game?"

"That wasn't me. Devlin did that."

"But you know how it's done? How the marks are chosen? How the game is rigged?"

O'Toole nodded. "Liam has watchers at every poker table in the city. When a pigeon is spotted, a middleman goes in and invites him to a real high-class, big-money game. Liam uses a banker from across the river with an eye for young boys. I set up a bar and pretty-up a few girls to bat their eyes and shake their teats at the pigeon. I also bring in food and sometimes a coon to play the piano. Can't stand that ragtime tripe, but it makes the girls bounce and jiggle more. The other players are our lads, scrubbed and polished to look like gents from out of town, travelers passing through, like. The dealer is our man too."

O'Toole drew on his cigar and cocked his head to the right. "The game starts out small and goes all evening. One of the guys gets caught bluffing a couple times, plays with his watch fob when he does. The pigeon wins more than he loses, but just enough to whet his appetite."

"Marked deck?" Falken said.

O'Toole nodded with a grin of admiration. "Our man's so good, I can't catch him dealing off the bottom. Around midnight, the pigeon wins several small pots in a row. He's feeling lucky. Then the big hand is dealt. The pigeon gets four kings, and our bluffer raises the stakes.

Just to make sure the trap is set, whichever girl catches the mark's eye goes over and whispers in his ear, 'He fingers his watch chain when he's bluffing.' Can always tell by their eyes they've swallowed the bait.

"With Garrett, once every dollar on the table was wagered, our man tossed in a deed to a Texas oilfield. It's a good forgery that cost a lot. Anyway, it did the trick. Garrett asked for a marker. There was a big discussion about it. Our bluffer made a show of not trusting him, demanding cash on the barrelhead or a deed of equal value. Finally an agreement was made, and our bluffer turned over a straight flush."

O'Toole laughed. "The look on Garrett's face was worth all the whiskey in Ireland. The bluffer demanded payment by sundown the next day, or he'd go to the police. When Garrett came back the next day empty-handed, Liam stepped in and offered him a way out. He pounced on the opportunity to save himself public humiliation. The rest started from there."

Falken nodded. "Yes, we know about the rest. What was being smuggled?"

"Whiskey and opium. Liam had a gang making bootleg laudanum. He also supplied just about every opium den from Kansas City to Pittsburgh."

"Is that why he murdered Garrett, because the smuggling operation fell apart?"

O'Toole's head snapped up and his eyes went wide. "Don't know nothing about no murder. My job's running whores and taking care of the game."

"Where is Devlin now?"

"I don't know."

"I promised you no harm provided you tell the truth. Lie to me—"

"I swear it by the Holy Mother, I don't know where he is. He's the boss. I don't ask about his business."

"Where is the laudanum distillery?"

"A farm in St. Charles County, north bank of the Missouri, but he shut it down when the ingredients dried up."

"If you had to get an urgent message to Devlin, how would you do it?"

"If Liam killed a rich man, what do you think he'd do to me?"

"You'll hang as an accomplice to murder if you don't cooperate fully."

O'Toole hugged himself and rocked gently, shaking his head. The tears returned, and he looked up. "Clancy's Tavern, south side near the levee. I leave word there, and Liam comes here by noon the next day."

"Who else would know where he is?"

"I don't know."

"Does he frequent any particular entertainment houses?"

"He's smitten with a whore. She works at a house on the east side, the Tipperary Social Club, but everyone calls it Mrs. Bannon's."

"Her name?" Falken said, as Sarah's face flashed into his mind.

"I don't know. He just calls her his green-eyed beauty."

Standing in the empty lobby, Falken relayed the information to Captain Morrissey. He briefly considered holding back the part involving the Tipperary, but integrity compelled him to be forthright.

"I'll have some men watch Clancy's, but as sure as God made little green apples, Devlin knows, or will shortly, about this raid. He'll not come near this place again," Morrissey said. He scratched his chin. "The whore might know something. Some men can be chatty afterward, but that's your inquiry to pursue. I've got to finish here and report to the chief. After that, I'll wire the St. Charles County sheriff about the distillery."

"We're going back to Garrett's home. Someone should warn them about the impending foreclosures. And the staff need to be interviewed before they leave."

"Shouldn't we maintain our pursuit of Devlin?" Westfall asked.

Falken shook his head. "He's a cautious criminal and he won't resume his normal routines immediately. Mrs. Bannon and her girls won't disappear overnight, but Garrett's domestic staff might."

"Well, you'll have to use the trolleys or hire a carriage, because I need mine," Morrissey said, then he left the hotel.

Falken noticed his aide's disappointment. "Investigating is a tedious process," he said in consolation. "A case can often turn on the slightest, seemingly insignificant detail."

"Yes, Major. Our task is to collect and analyze the facts, all of the facts, and follow the leads to a logical conclusion."

Falken grinned and clapped Westfall on the shoulder. "So you *do* pay attention."

CHAPTER ELEVEN

Falken rang the doorbell.

Adams opened the door and recognition dawned. "Good afternoon, Major Falken."

"Hello, Adams. I need to speak with you."

"Of course, sir. Please come in." Adams stood aside to admit Falken and Westfall, then closed the door and led the way to the gentlemen's parlor.

When the trio was seated, Falken said, "We need to speak with the staff, but I want tell you something first." He spent a few minutes detailing the depths of Garrett's financial woes.

"Three months?" Adams said, with shocked disbelief.

"Possibly. I suspect it will unfold quicker than that." Falken gave the butler a minute to absorb the news, then he chronicled the real version of Garrett's travels on Saturday.

"I knew him for forty years," Adams said. "In all that time, it never entered my mind he would lie to me. Where was he all those Saturdays he claimed to be with Mr. Decker?"

"Did he have a mistress?"

Adams massaged his temples. "Ten minutes ago I would've fiercely denied your suggestion. Now I just don't know. I suppose it's possible."

"Are the staff all here today?"

"All but the kitchenmaid. She hasn't returned." Adams looked at Falken. "Please don't tell them about the foreclosures. I know lying is a sin, but I'm thinking about Margaret and the children."

Falken nodded. "Did your son drive Garrett?"

"Occasionally, but Charles preferred to leave his carriage for Margaret. During the week a man from Garrett House picked him up."

"How did Garrett leave here Saturday?"

"A neighbor, Mr. Quinn, offered a ride downtown in his motorcar."

"We'll begin with your son anyway."

Adams stood, straightened his frock coat, resumed his public persona, and left the room.

⧗

Short interviews with Adams' son, wife, the housekeeper, gardener, cook, and chambermaid had been fruitless. They all did their jobs without concerning themselves with their employer's affairs. All displayed varying degrees of empathy or apathy toward the family, but they were mainly concerned with their own lives and future.

Adams ushered in Gretchen, the parlormaid, and closed the door.

"Please, sit down," Falken said, pointing to a chair opposite his own.

The young blonde crossed the room and sat on the chair's edge, hands crossed on her lap, eyes downcast.

Falken couldn't help looking at her for a moment. The resemblance was more than vague: she could have been Anna's sister.

It looked like she'd been crying. Crying? Her reaction to Garrett's death seemed extreme, passionate, disproportionate. None of the other members of staff seemed to be grieving except Adams and his wife.

Something on the parlormaid's apron sparkled, catching his eye. A fine pendant watch. It looked expensive, and was certainly worth more than a maid could afford.

Westfall cleared his throat.

Falken glanced at his aide, then back to the parlormaid. "What is your full name, Gretchen?"

She did not look at him. "Gretchen Heinen," she said with a Bavarian accent.

"How long have you worked here?"

"Ten, no, eleven months."

"How old are you?"

"Nineteen."

"Where is your family?"

"*Mutti und Papa* … excuse me, Mother and Father died of cholera."

"Brothers or sisters?"

"Hannah and Ursula died before I was born. I haven't seen Erich in several years, but he sends a letter every Christmas. He went to South Africa to dig for gold."

"That's a very nice pendant watch. A gift?"

Gretchen doubled over, held her face, and sobbed.

Damn, I was right, he thought. Falken crossed to her side, gently straightened her up and handed over his handkerchief. Gretchen wiped her red-rimmed eyes and struggled to regain her composure.

Falken remained at her side and placed his left hand on her shoulder. "Garrett gave you the watch?"

She nodded.

"You were his mistress?"

Another nod.

"How long?"

She sniffled and replied, "It st-st-started a few w-weeks after I-I came to work h-here."

"When Garrett claimed to be in Belleville overnight, he was with you?"

"*Ja.*" Gretchen nodded again.

"And you were with him this past Saturday night?"

She tensed and wailed again, rocking back and forth.

The door opened and Falken turned. Adams stood there with a quizzical expression, but did not enter. After a long moment, realization dawned; the butler's eyes narrowed, and he closed the door.

Falken looked down at Gretchen's sobbing, trembling form; this was more than lover's grief. For her to be so distraught ... My God, he thought. Is this child a murderess?

He spoke in a stern, commanding tone. "Look at me, girl."

Slowly, Gretchen raised her chin to meet his gaze. Her eyes conveyed a myriad of emotions.

"Do you know how Garrett died?"

She convulsed and gasped, "H-h-he was alive when I left."

"Alive, but injured?"

She nodded rapidly. "*Ja*, y-yes."

"Tell me everything. *Everything.*" Falken sat down and looked at Westfall, gesturing toward the liquor cabinet.

Westfall rose and selected a bottle of bourbon. He poured two fingers in a crystal tumbler and carried it to Gretchen. She shook her head, but he pushed the heavy glass into her hand. Then he reseated himself and picked up the journal.

"It'll calm your nerves," coaxed Falken. Strange advice from a teetotaler, he thought.

Gretchen wiped her eyes again and sipped the amber liquid. Though her face contorted, she emptied the tumbler with several more sips. Then she put the glass aside and blew her nose.

"Ch-Charles was attracted to me from the d-day I arrived." She took another moment to steel herself. "Everyone thinks I'm just a naive girl, but I saw the way he looked at me. He made a point of coming into whatever room I was working in and watching me. It was a grand game. I teased him by bending over a lot, or leaning over him to clean something. I lost my balance and fell into him a few times. I was coy and giggly, and he grinned like a little boy. Sometimes he'd break my fall by putting his hands on my breasts."

She looked at Falken's chair. "The first time he took me was in this room, on that chair. It was awful. He hurt me. But when it was over, I longed to do it again. And we did, at every opportunity. In here, in his study, the garden, the carriage house, wherever we could steal a few minutes of privacy. I worried Adams or that bitch Mrs. Fuchs would catch us, but I trusted Charles to protect me."

She looked down at the pendant and ran her fingers over it. "The Saturday before Christmas, he gave me this watch and told me to meet him at the House on Market Street at seven o'clock. I arrived to a wonderful surprise. He had converted one of the ground-floor storerooms into a room just for us. There was a brass bed, washbasin, mirror, bathtub, and a wardrobe with lacy French undergarments. It was beautiful. He told me I could keep some things there, and go there anytime I wished. He gave me a key."

"A key?"

"Yes, the room is around back. There's a door that opens into the alley." Gretchen unbuttoned her collar and pulled out a gold necklace strung through a Yale key. She clutched the key in her fingers, like a talisman.

"Go on," Falken said.

"Whenever Charles wanted to meet at our room, he'd leave a book, *Anna Karenina*, on his reading table in the library. Saturday morning, when he departed, the book was there. So I dressed and left the house.

I waited all day for him. It was nearly seven when he came in. I could tell he was in a foul mood, but so was I. I'd been there for hours. It was hot, I was hungry, I needed a bath, and I desperately needed to have him."

"You were there all day? Garrett House is not open for business on Saturdays?"

"Men were working. I could hear them moving about, but no one paid me any attention. The windows are curtained, and the inside door is barred, with a keep-out sign. Everyone there pretends that room doesn't exist. I snapped at him for making me wait. He bit back, and we had an argument. I demanded he take me to a restaurant for supper; he protested about indiscretion; I accused him of being ashamed of me. It went on for some time. When our anger was spent, he told me to take a bath while he went out to get us something to eat. But I waited. He returned with a bottle of wine, bread, and roasted chicken. We ate and bathed together. Then we lay down."

She looked at the floor for a moment then looked up at Falken. "Afterward, Charles began telling me about his money troubles again. He had promised me that after all his accounts were settled we'd go away together, to San Francisco. We were going to make a new life there. He said he would open another brewery, and maybe a vineyard. We would have a lovely home by the sea, and everything would be perfect. I felt guilty about him leaving his children behind, but he didn't seem troubled by the thought.

"When he'd finished complaining about Decker interfering with his plans, I asked him when we'd be able to move west. He became angry again and accused me of being selfish. I protested, and we argued, again. When I thought it was over, I told him we had to go soon because I was pregnant."

Gretchen gazed at the ceiling with faraway, despondent eyes. "His face, his eyes, I'd never seen him look like that before. "He slapped me, kicked me onto the floor, and called me a whore. He said terrible things. He accused me of giving myself to other men, of lying to him and tricking him."

Tears spilled onto her cheeks again. "He said, 'No German whore is going to saddle me with a bastard.' Then he said he was going to kill me. I got up and ran to the door, but it was locked. He rose from the bed with hate in his eyes and reached for his coat. I was terrified. I knew he carried a gun in his coat pocket because he'd shown it to me. I backed into the corner by the door, and my hand touched the bat."

"Bat? Baseball bat?"

"*Ja*, there's a wagonhouse across the alley. One of the drivers, Heinie, loves baseball. He always keeps a bat, ball and glove under his seat. One day I took the bat and put it in the room, for defense, in case anyone tried to break in when I was there alone. I gripped the bat, ran at Charles, and hit him on the head. I was scared and hurt and angry. I hit him again. The bat split, and he fell to the floor, groaning, bleeding. My God, I thought. What have I done? I dropped the broken bat and tried to go to him, but he kicked me away. He pulled his wallet from the coat. That's all he had in his pocket, not a gun. He took my letter from the wallet and threw it at me. Then he threw money on the floor. He said, 'There, you stinking whore, take everything that's yours and go away.'"

"What letter was that?" Falken asked.

Gretchen wiped her eyes and cheeks. "After Charles promised to take me to San Francisco, I wrote him a letter. I put all of my feelings for him and our future on paper. The next day I slipped the envelope into the stack of mail just before Adams took it to him."

Falken nodded.

"I couldn't believe what was happening. He hit me, threatened my life, called me filthy names, rejected our child, and I hit him. I hurt my *Liebling*."

She buried her face in her hands, then shook her head and went on. "I gathered up my clothing, shoes, handbag and key, and unlocked the door. I ran out, crying. I went into the wagonhouse, dressed myself in the dark and returned here. I know I injured his head, but I swear he was alive when I ran out. Did I kill him?"

Falken thought for several moments. If she's lying, he thought, she's the best damn actor in the world. Her emotions seemed raw and genuine. He didn't believe she was aware of the stabbing. He didn't think she had lied, or omitted anything of substance. She had confessed her sins, and he didn't feel he had the right to deny her absolution.

"No, you didn't kill him," he said. "Someone else did that."

Gretchen's expression changed from horrified guilt to deep sadness.

"Why did you return here?" he asked her.

"*Mutti* used to say that bad things always look better in the morning. I hoped we could apologize to each other. I hoped he would think about the baby, and we could still go to San Francisco."

"Did you take back your letter?"

"No, I gave him my love with that letter. I couldn't take it back."

"Did you see anyone in the alleyway or nearby when you left the building?"

"No."

"What time did you leave?"

"I'm not sure. It was nearly one when I got back here. I know that because the rain had just started. I walked, so it took maybe three-quarters of an hour."

"Did Garrett mention any names? Did you get the sense that he was afraid of anyone? Was anyone causing problems for him?"

"Charles wasn't afraid of any man. He was angry with the steamboat man, Decker, but he didn't mention any other."

"Have you seen a doctor, Gretchen? Are you certain you're with child?"

"I don't have money for a doctor, but I'm sure. A woman knows these things."

"What are you going to do? Is there anyone you can turn to for help?"

Gretchen shook her head. "I don't know anyone here. I'll keep working until the pregnancy is obvious and I'm discharged. We haven't been paid in some time, but at least I have food and a bed."

Falken took out his wallet and withdrew a card. He took the pen from Westfall and wrote on the back. Then he stood, handed the card to Gretchen and said, "This is a home for unwed mothers. They'll see you through your confinement and arrange a suitable home for the child." Then he held out his hand. "I need the key."

Gretchen clutched the key in her left hand and covered her abdomen with her right. "*Nein*. This key and the baby inside of me are all I have left of Charles."

"That key is just a piece of brass, nothing more. It doesn't hold any memories." Falken tapped his fingers on his temple and chest. "Those are in here. As for the child, without a husband both of you would be condemned to a life of poverty. Have you seen the tenements and shacks near the levee?"

Gretchen stared mutely in response.

"Is that what you want for your baby? Endless years of privation and squalor?"

Her eyes lit up. "Charles's estate. They won't give a tinker's damn about me, but surely provision will be made for Charles's offspring."

Falken shook his head. "There is no estate. He was mired in debt. Mrs. Garrett and her children are penniless. They don't know it yet, but in a month, maybe less, they'll be dependent on charity."

"*Nein*! There must be money. He planned to take me away. He said—"

"There is no money. Garrett had been surviving on credit and it was exhausted. He couldn't have purchased a barrel of his own beer. I'm sorry, but that is the truth."

Defiance gave way to disbelief, then sorrow. Tears flowing again, Gretchen shook her head, removed the key from around her neck, and dropped it in Falken's hand. Then she stood and ran from the room.

CHAPTER TWELVE

In the alley behind Garrett House Falken mounted a set of movable steps, turned a doorknob and pushed, but the door didn't move. "Someone thought to lock up on the way out."

"Yes, but who?" Westfall said.

Falken inserted the key into the Yale lock, turned it and pushed the door inward. The familiar stench of stale blood and rotting flesh stung his nostrils.

Westfall turned away and backed up a step. Covering his mouth and nose with his handkerchief, he said, "Christ, that's awful."

After carefully examining the threshold and adjacent floor, Falken stepped inside.

Directly ahead was an interior door, barred with iron straps fastened to the jamb. Lining the far wall were a rack of coat pegs, wardrobe, washbasin with mirror, and a large porcelain tub. A woman's cloak hung on one of the pegs. The wardrobe's mirrored doors stood open, revealing an ample supply of lacy French undergarments.

The basin appeared to have a smear of blood on the top edge. A small table and two chairs were on the near left wall. Flies buzzed over and around two plates of chicken bones, a partial loaf of bread, a nearly empty wine bottle, and a pair of water glasses. Standing along the near right wall were a smaller wardrobe and a valet stand.

Centered on the back wall was a brass bed. Flies hovered over and crawled on it. Even from across the room, crimson stains were visible. A pool of apparently dried blood was on the floor next to the bed.

The only things missing from Gretchen's description were the broken bat, her letter, and Garrett's cash. Falken knew he could have put the money and letter back in his wallet. That would have been the sensible thing to do, but Garrett wasn't the kind of man who cleans a room, certainly not the type to sweep up wood splinters from a shattered baseball bat. Except for the pool of dried blood, the floor was spotless.

Falken backed out of the room into fresh air, descended the steps, and turned his back to the open door.

Westfall was leaning against the adjacent wagon house. "Never thought I'd appreciate the stink of horse dung," he said.

"Go out to Market and flag a policeman. Tell him I need Captain Morrissey here at once."

Westfall crossed the alley and dropped the satchel next to the open door, then hobbled away as quickly as his game leg allowed.

An hour later, a police carriage and two mounted patrolmen entered the alley from the east end. Falken, sitting on his haunches, stood and waved.

The carriage braked to a stop, and Morrissey hopped down. "What's this?"

"The murder scene," Falken replied.

Morrissey stopped in mid-stride and shook his head. "Major, I'll never understand how you do it. Anything inside?"

"Plenty of blood. I decided to wait for you before making a thorough search."

Morrissey nodded and sniffed the air. "Smells like a slaughterhouse, but they always do." He motioned to the mounted patrolmen. "Post at both ends of the alley," he told them. Then he looked at his driver and pointed to the wagonhouse bay door. "Over there, no one comes into the alleyway."

Morrissey went up the steps and into the room. He pointed at the furnishings. "Looks like a flophouse." He faced the table. "Somebody ate here?"

"I'll explain when we're finished," Falken replied.

Morrissey shrugged.

The three men began searching, making a mental inventory of the room's contents.

Falken examined three sizable bloodstains on the bedsheet. Disturbed flies rose from the bed and buzzed noisily around his head. The largest stain was at the foot of the bed. An unsoiled strip of bedding separated two smaller, dark splotches near the head.

Falken moved to the left side and studied the dried pool of blood on the floor. Turning his head, he saw a trail of blood spots and light smears extending several feet toward the door. He had missed these earlier in the shadowy darkness, but now each stood out clearly when viewed from within the room. After a full minute, he stepped to the end of the blood trail, five feet from the door.

"Garrett was first stabbed here," he said.

Morrissey and Westfall stopped what they were doing to listen.

Falken walked slowly toward the bed. "He reeled backward, while the killer continued to strike." He pointed to drops of blood at his feet. "Again and again and again and again. A frenzied flurry of thrusts to the abdomen."

He stopped on the left side of the bed, clear of the dried pool. "Dr. Evans's report states that the five chest wounds penetrated at a much sharper upward angle than the abdominal wounds. Garrett fell onto the bed with the killer on top of him, still striking in a straight underhand motion."

Falken mimed thrusting a blade at standing and horizontal targets to demonstrate the different angles of attack. Then he pointed to the separated bloodstains. "It happened there. Garrett lay on his back, blood running down his sides onto the bed. The killer stood, and Garrett sat up, tried to rise, and collapsed facedown here." He pointed to the large stain.

"How can you be sure of that?" Westfall said, gasping and shooing flies.

"There's no logical reason for the killer to move him from one end of the bed to the other. No, Garrett was trying to escape or fight back, and collapsed and died right there." Falken pointed to the large stain again. "It's the biggest and darkest. Blood pumped out of his body and soaked the bed."

He indicated the dried pool of blood on the floor. "After Garrett died, the killer pulled him onto the floor and left him there for a considerable length of time. Long enough for that much blood to drain from his wounds."

"Why put him on the floor?" Morrissey said.

"Only the killer knows the reason."

"But what was the killer doing during that considerable length of time?" Westfall said.

"He was across the alleyway hitching a team and wagon to transport the corpse," Falken said.

Morrissey shook his head. "The bay door is secured at night with a heavy chain stretched across the opening to prevent a wagon passing through."

"Smuggling and other nefarious activities are best done after dark. You can bet Devlin has a key to the padlock."

Morrissey shrugged and nodded in reply.

Westfall's face was screwed up in thought and discomfort. "How was the body moved from here," he said, pointing at the floor, "to the door without smearing the floor with blood?"

Falken indicated the bed with his chin. "The top sheet is missing. The sheet was laid on the floor, and the corpse rolled onto it and dragged to the door." He described a course that went around the blood drops with his finger. "The threshold is the right height from the ground. The steps could've been moved aside, a stake bed wagon pulled up sideways to the door, and the corpse simply dragged onto it."

Falken moved over to the washbasin. "With so many wounds inflicted up close, the killer was certainly splattered with blood. So once the corpse was loaded, he stood here to wash his face and hands." He gestured to the blood smear on the basin's top edge and a red-stained hand towel.

Next he moved to the coat rack. "A cloak for a lady, but nothing for a gentleman." He pointed to the far-right peg. "The empty pegs are all dusty, except this one. One of Garrett's coats hung here. The killer took it to cover his bloody clothing. Then he walked out, closed the door, and used Garrett's key to turn the lock, thus concealing the murder scene."

"And emptied the rest of his pockets because that's what criminals do," Morrissey added. "Now explain what you know about the rest of it." He nodded at the table and the feminine accoutrements.

Falken led the way back outside. "Garrett's parlormaid, Gretchen Heinen, was also his mistress," he said.

He spent the next half hour recounting the interview, and answering Morrissey's numerous questions. When he had finished, Morrissey was pacing around in a small circle, hands on his hips.

"I don't see how you can be so sure she wasn't involved," Morrissey said. "It's as plain as the nose on your face that he was stringing her along. A bastard on the way? No money? No family to turn to? Sure to lose her job and be out on the street? That's a wagonload of motive for revenge. And you can be sure Devlin was watching and knew about her. He offers a small purse, she bangs Garrett on the head to stun him and unlocks the door."

"You weren't there during the interview. I saw her demeanor and emotion; it wasn't faked."

"Major, please. Manipulating well-to-do gentlemen is Gretchen Heinen's real trade. She admitted hitting him with the bat, for Christ's sake."

"We must disagree on this point. I believe her."

Morrissey snorted. "We'll see. After Devlin's caught, I'll interrogate her myself." He motioned to his driver and mounted the carriage.

After Morrissey and the mounted police had gone, Westfall said, "Major, where's the broken bat and letter?"

"I don't know. Perhaps Garrett picked them up, or the killer removed them."

"Why would he? The killer, I mean. After all, they would be of no interest or consequence to someone not connected to Miss Heinen. An unrelated murderer would cover his own tracks, not hers."

Falken removed his homburg and scratched his head. "I don't know—yet. But I will uncover the truth."

"Even if it sends her to the gallows?"

The increasingly familiar tingle ran down Falken's spine. Distracted by the sensation, he turned back toward the door.

"We … we must make a detailed diagram of the interior of the room. Note the position of every item, every speck of blood." He paused to glance up and down the alley. "And we must include annotations describing the sequence of events I laid out."

Westfall folded his handkerchief and tied it, like a mask, over his mouth and nose. Then, reluctantly, he picked up the satchel and went inside.

Falken turned in a slow circle, looking up and down. *I can feel your eyes. But where are you? Who are you? What is your purpose?*

Westfall called out a question, breaking the spell. Falken scanned the rooftops, then turned and went inside as late afternoon shadows crept along the alley.

CHAPTER THIRTEEN

A fusillade of gunshots rang out from the hills. The sergeant major's head exploded, coating nearby men and horses in a thick, red-gray goo; Captain Searles clutched his chest and fell out of the saddle, writhing; a quartermaster's orderly fell from his wagon seat and did not move again; a hard-charging corporal somersaulted backward off his mount, landed hard and screamed in agony; a pair of horses whinnied and collapsed, legs thrashing, entrails spilling out, riders pinned underneath.

The column scattered in all directions. Frightened men and horses scurried over open, featureless ground seeking escape.

He dismounted, gave his horse a hard slap on the rump and yelled, "Get!"

All around him, men fell screaming, kicking, and then lay motionless. Puffs of gunsmoke and muzzle flashes from the hills continued unabated.

He had to get control of the battle: get the men into cover, organize a coordinated defense, and counterattack. He searched for good ground as bullets thudded and ricocheted around him. There, the base of that hill on the left. There were good-sized rocks and a deep gully.

"Men, move left! Everyone, move left! Bugler, color sergeant, come with me."

Revolver drawn, left hand gripping his saber scabbard, he ran for the rocks. The men obeyed his command, some on foot, others on horseback. His head and eyes were moving constantly as he ran. He saw more troopers fall. Hitched horses and mules bucked and kicked, and some went down. Frightened, riderless mounts galloped in confused circles.

Ahead, a group of men had reached the gully.

Yes. Get in there boys. Find good positions and we'll—

A fiery booming explosion threw them into the air; smoke and dust billowed upward and outward.

Noooooo!

Men and parts of men rained down on the rocks. Other men, running and riding toward the rocks, continued to fall.

Goddamn it! Stop killing my men.

An unseen, burning fist punched him in the chest. He went down hard, and the world turned black.

Head throbbing, chest on fire, he came to with his arms tied behind his back. A booted foot kicked him again. His head snapped sideways. His eyes fluttered. The world was a spinning blur. He couldn't focus. Sounds were distorted. The air was heavy with woodsmoke and the scent of roasting meat.

Then everything settled and became more or less clear. Firelight glowed in the darkness. Indians, and white men dressed like Indians, moved to and fro. Women talked while children ran and laughed. Unseen men moaned and sobbed. He felt cool ground under him, something hard and unyielding behind.

A hand grabbed his hair and jerked his head back. "You still with us?" The unseen rasping voice was close to his right ear. The man's breath was foul. His stink was worse.

Another voice from the right: "Colonel, he's awake."

A tall shadow approached, marching with a purpose. Two shorter shadows flanked the first, matching his cadence. They moved into the firelight and stopped several feet away from him.

He recognized the tall man in the center, despite his strange appearance. He had a long, full, dark beard. He wore a cavalry officer's hat, and a buckskin shirt decorated with rough beads, animal claws and bits of bone. An officer's belt and yellow sash was wrapped around his waist, and a saber with scabbard hung from the belt. Yellow-striped officer's trousers disappeared into knee-high cactus moccasins.

The shorter men were similarly dressed. A white man stood at the right, an Indian at the left. Both had U.S. Army-issued sabers and holstered sidearms attached to their belts.

The tall man stared with dull, lifeless eyes. The gaze seemed to bore right through him without seeing. Finally the tall man spoke. "I'm Colonel Nathaniel Hawkins, and you're my prisoner." After a moment, the eyes moved.

The stinking man, still pulling his hair, slapped his burning chest. "The colonel addressed you. Regulations require that you reply with courtesy and respect."

A sharp pain stabbed through him from shoulder to bowel. He grunted and said, "Yes, Colonel, I am your prisoner."

Colonel Hawkins smiled with dead eyes. "I see you're a hard man. You won't break easy." He nodded slowly. "That's okay, I respect courage. Hell, if you survive this I might even allow you to join my army."

Hawkins nodded to his aides. "Get it started, gentlemen. No need to keep the brave captain waiting."

The aides turned and marched away. Hawkins stepped aside.

A teenaged trooper, stripped naked, was dragged into the light. His outstretched arms were tied to two posts driven into the hard dry ground. He had been severely beaten. Tears flowed from eyes that were swollen shut, and he trembled with fear.

Two Indians marched up to the boy; one held a sharpened deer antler, the other a crude flint knife.

"Brave captain, before we begin I'd like to know your name."

His hair was jerked sharply.

"Captain Herbert Falken, Engineer Corps, United States Army."

"Engineers? Really? I think I should feel insulted. The army doesn't even have the decency to send a line officer to kill me."

Men and women, seen and unseen, laughed.

"Nonetheless, brave Captain Falken, you're here on a fool's errand. And now your men are going to pay for that foolishness. My only regret is that the generals who sent you aren't here to share your misery."

Hawkins raised his right arm.

The Indians moved forward.

The trooper let out an agonizing shriek. It went on and on, ringing in Falken's ears and piercing his soul.

Nooooooo!

"Major! Major!"

Hands shook him. He leapt to his feet and grappled with his attacker. Fight through the enemy and escape. His eyes focused, and Westfall's red face came into view. He was horrified to realize his right hand was clamped on his aide's throat, while his left struggled to throw punches. He jumped back, letting his arms drop.

The light was on. Westfall leaned against the wall, clad in a nightshirt, rubbing his throat and panting.

"I … heard you … calling out. You were having … a nightmare, so I came in to … wake you." His eyes were wary, face drawn. He took several deep breaths. "It's been some time since you've had one that bad. I forgot about not touching you. I'm sorry."

Falken sat on the edge of the bed and held up his hand. "You have nothing to be sorry about. I owe you an apology. It's not your fault my nights are haunted by ghosts. Did I hurt you?"

"No, your reaction just took me by surprise. As I said, it's been a while."

Falken looked at his watch: four-ten. "I'm sorry. Try to get some more sleep."

Westfall nodded and padded back to his room across the second-floor hallway.

Unwilling to risk a repeat performance, Falken rose, switched off the light and left his room. As quietly as possible, he ascended the attic stairs and crept along the upper hallway. Owen was asleep in his room and didn't deserve to be awakened because of his employer's demons. At the end of the hallway, he opened a door and mounted the tower stairs. On the landing, French doors opened onto a small balcony, but he turned and went up to the tower proper.

Standing in what was essentially a small belfry, minus any bells, he breathed in the cool night air. His hair, exposed skin, and nightshirt were damp with perspiration. A chill ran from head to toe, but he endured it. The prickly sensation cleared his head.

After several minutes, he moved a chair, which had been placed in the tower for nights like this, to the eastern opening and sat. He opened a worn humidor and picked out a cigar. Once it was lit, he put his feet up on the sill, drew deeply, and settled in to wait for sunrise.

Ghostly images dancing through his head provided familiar unwelcome company.

CHAPTER FOURTEEN

Dressed in crisply creased gray trousers and jacket with a black vest, burgundy necktie, and his new boots, Falken entered the dining room.

Westfall was in his usual chair reading the *Post-Dispatch*. Owen was pouring coffee.

"Good morning, Major. Mrs. Howard will have breakfast ready in a few minutes," Owen said, and left the room.

Westfall looked up. "Good morning, Major."

Falken took his seat and said, "Good morning, Westfall. I hope you can forgive me."

"Forgiven and forgotten."

Falken nodded, and sipped his coffee. "What's happening on this Wednesday, according to Mr. Pulitzer?"

Westfall lowered the paper. "The Perfectos beat Washington yesterday, eight to three. The Spiders are still being mauled by everyone."

Falken shook his head. "Cleveland would be better off without a baseball team. They've lost more than a hundred games."

"A hundred and twenty, and all but one away game."

"What else is happening?" Falken said with a snort.

"The hurricane that hit Puerto Rico and the Bahama Islands is apparently going to strike North Carolina next. And British relations with South Africa continue to deteriorate."

"Boers, Zulus, Mahdis, fuzzy-wuzzies, and Dervishes." Falken shook his head. "Africa is no good for Britain. They would be best advised to content themselves with India. There, they have an established bureaucracy and a wealth of commercial resources. Africa is too wild, with too many unknowns. Every time they turn around, another tribe is rising up and declaring war." He thrust a finger in the air. "Chinese Gordon went to his death at Khartoum for nothing."

"African diamonds and gold would be good for them."

"The Boers are not going to step aside and say, 'Here, take it.' I was in my plebe year when they fought the Boers the first time. Those backward Dutch farmers trounced them."

"Surely the British has to maintain a foothold to secure Suez. Without the canal, how would they profit from India?"

"Johannesburg is a long way from Suez."

"Not if Mr. Rhodes has his way. He's still promoting his idea for a transcontinental railroad from Cape Town to Cairo."

Falken shook his head again. "Name a colony after a man, and he thinks he owns the whole damned continent. Cecil Rhodes and his ilk will agitate until they have their war."

"What about the rights of British citizens in South Africa and Orange Free State?"

"If a Briton came here today, could he vote in next year's election? Of course not. Would we demand that the laws change to accommodate him?"

"But Kruger is denying—"

Mrs. Howard entered carrying two plates piled with eggs, fried potatoes, bacon, and biscuits. Owen followed with a butter dish and bowl of blackberry jam.

"Good morning, Mrs. Howard. That smells wonderful," Falken said.

"Thank you, Major. Your eye looks better this morning." Mrs. Howard set a plate in front of each man, beaming like a proud mother.

After Owen had placed the dish and bowl, Mrs. Howard said, "Luke, go eat yours before it gets cold." She turned to Westfall. "I don't know who Kruger is, but never mind him and eat your breakfast."

She rolled her eyes, reached around him, and snatched the newspaper off the table. "Mr. James, I've told you before, the ink comes off and stains the tablecloth." She left the room muttering. "They think I've got nothing better to do than wash that tablecloth every day. Lord, help me."

Westfall looked sheepish.

Falken buttered a biscuit and chuckled. "What would we do without her?"

"Starve or suffer endlessly with Owen's cooking. Given a choice, I think I'd rather keep Mrs. Howard."

With both men chuckling and digging into their food, the gate buzzer sounded in the kitchen.

Mrs. Howard walked heavily down the hallway, reaching the front door just as the bell rang. After a moment, she appeared in the dining room doorway. "I'm sorry, Major, there's a messenger boy who says he has a letter he can only hand to you."

Falken put down his fork, wiped his mouth with a linen napkin, and stood. "The boy is just following his instructions."

Mrs. Howard headed back to the kitchen and Falken strode to the open front door.

A scruffy teenaged boy dressed in baggy clothing stood on the porch, clutching his soft cap in his left hand and an envelope in his right. "Are you Major Falken, sir?"

"I am. What do you have there?"

Falken pulled a nickel from his pocket and stepped across the threshold. The familiar tingle ran down his spine.

The crack of splintering wood above his head made Falken duck instinctively. He recognized the sounds of a near miss even before the boom of the rifle report reached his ears. Lunging forward, he grabbed the boy by his shirt and reeled backward into the house. A second bullet tore through the oak door and thudded into the plaster wall behind them. Falken dropped to the floor, covering the boy with his body, and kicked the door closed.

"Gunfire!" he yelled. "Take cover."

A plate crashed to the floor in the dining room.

Westfall scrambled into the hallway, saw the damaged door and yelled, "Owen, arm yourself! Mrs. Howard, go the cellar and stay there." Then he bent down to Falken. "My God, are you hurt?"

From the kitchen came the sound of Owen's boots pounding up the service stairs, and Mrs. Howard's muffled voice exclaiming and praying.

Falken rolled off the wide-eyed boy. "No, two clean misses." He crab-walked to the door and turned the lock. "Take him," he said, pointing at the boy, "to the library and stay with him."

Westfall pulled the scared, whimpering youth up by his collar and moved toward the back of the house.

Seconds later, Owen charged down the main staircase armed with his Spanish Mauser. He had brought home the bolt-action rifle, among other souvenirs, from Cuba. The young orderly looked to his employer for orders.

"Be careful with that. I'm certain the excitement is past," Falken said.

As he walked down the hallway to the telephone, Owen positioned himself between Falken and the door, rifle held at port arms.

When an operator came on the crackling line, Falken said, "Police headquarters, Captain Morrissey, please."

An hour and a half later, Falken stood in his library, a cigar clenched in his teeth. He stared absentmindedly at a print of *Victory at Yorktown*. Morrissey was interrogating the messenger boy while Westfall recorded every word in efficient shorthand. Owen stood guard at the door; his Spanish rifle now replaced by a strange-looking handgun. Policemen were outside searching Tower Grove Park for anything unusual.

"No one here is going to harm you, boy. Just tell the truth," Morrissey said.

The youth was seated on a chair in the middle of the room. Wide-eyed, he nodded rapidly.

"Who gave you the envelope?"

"A man."

"What did he look like?"

"A little shorter than you and thinner. Red hair, beard, hard eyes. He wore a black derby and an emerald-green suit."

"Where were you?"

The boy looked at the floor, bowed his head, and crossed his arms.

"What were you doing, boy?" Morrissey asked gruffly.

"Filching potatoes from an old man's wagon, over by the Arsenal." The youth looked up, teary-eyed. "Dad left, and Mom can't feed all of us. I was just taking care of my own."

"What happened?"

"The man grabbed us by the collar as we were walking away, my little brother and me. Said he was going to call a cop. I begged him not to. Then he said he'd let us go if I did a job for him. He handed me the letter, and told me where to go and what to say. I gave the spuds to my little brother and told him to run home. Then the man flipped me a half dollar and said he'd be watching to make sure I did the job. But I swear I didn't know anything about shooting."

"Did you see the man following you?"

The boy shook his head. "No. But I guess he would've had to get ahead of me so he was ready to shoot when I rang the bell. Unless he had a partner, but I didn't see anyone else."

Satisfied the boy had told all, Morrissey crumpled the plain envelope and blank sheet of paper and tossed both into a wastepaper basket. "All right, boy, run along home now." He towered over the youth and shook his finger. "But no more filching. You steal so much as a grain of salt and I'll give you a sound thrashing."

Without hesitation, the youth bolted from the room and ran for the front door.

"Well, he gave a good description. It sure sounds like Devlin to me," Morrissey said.

Falken remained silent.

"But wouldn't Devlin avoid exposing himself," Westfall said, "and delegate something like this to an underling?"

"Not likely," Morrissey said. "Devlin rules his gang and territory with fear and intimidation. Does all of his own killing and makes sure everyone knows it."

"Then why hasn't he been hanged for murder already?"

Morrissey shook his head. "Knowing what he's done and proving it are two different things. He's a wily animal with a knack for survival."

Falken blew a cloud of smoke at the ceiling. "Why?"

"Why what?" Westfall and Morrissey responded in unison.

"Why try to kill me? Even if I'm dead, the evidence against him still exists. Killing me doesn't serve any logical purpose."

Morrissey snorted. "Major, a thug on the run is like a cornered rat. He lashes out in desperation. Reason has little to do with it."

Falken turned to his companions and crossed his arms, cigar in his fingers. "I don't see that, at least not in this case. This is a meticulous man who plans everything down to the smallest detail: the merchant game, Garrett's blackmailing, the murder and disposal of the body. No, this kind of criminal does not act precipitously. Every action has a purpose and predetermined outcome."

Morrissey picked up his helmet. "Major, I thank the Almighty for your help, but sometimes that big brain of yours thinks too much. But once the red-headed rat is caught, I'll ask him why, just to satisfy you." He nodded and walked to the door. "Until then, I strongly suggest you arm yourselves when leaving the house. Better still, arm yourselves in the house as well." Then he exited the library and left the house.

"What do we do now?" Westfall said.

Falken pointed with his cigar. "Owen, what is that contraption you are wearing?"

Owen patted his shoulder holster, then drew and displayed his pistol. "I picked it up in Cuba, along with the rifle. It's a Mauser C-ninety-six. Some call it the Broomhandle." He pointed to the grip, which did resemble a broom handle. "It's a semiautomatic pistol and will shoot as fast as I can squeeze the trigger." He pulled a stripper clip from a pouch attached to the shoulder holster's chest strap. "It reloads the same as the rifle. Just fit the bottom of this clip into a slot in the open breech and press the cartridges into the magazine with your thumb. Takes some practice, but I can reload ten rounds in a couple seconds. Try doing that with a revolver."

"Is it accurate?"

Owen nodded. "Major, this pistol will outshoot your Merwin Hulbert and Mr. Westfall's service revolver. Outside Santiago, I saw three men killed at thirty yards with this pistol."

"Germans are always tinkering with something. To answer your question, we go on with our investigation. The only change is that from now on we'll all have a weapon within arm's reach at all times."

CHAPTER FIFTEEN

A four-passenger carriage, drawn by a pair of horses, stopped in front of the Tipperary Social Club. Falken and Westfall dismounted. Falken paid the driver and instructed him to wait. Both men went up the walkway and porch steps to the door.

After a short wait, a redhead dressed for house cleaning duty opened the door and waved them in. "I'll tell Mrs. Bannon you're here, Major. Make yourselves at home in the parlor."

Falken walked into the room with a feeling of foreboding. He longed to see Sarah again, but knew this meeting would not be pleasant.

A minute later, Sarah Bannon glided into the parlor, smiling, eyes bright, but after making eye contact with Falken, her expression became guarded. "Herbert, this certainly is a surprise." She went to Westfall and gave him a brief embrace. "It's good to see you again, James."

"Always a pleasure, Mrs. Bannon."

Hands clasped behind his back, Falken said, "Sarah, I regret this is not a social call."

She turned to her lover and met his gaze again. Her face was neutral, but her eyes burned with either passion or anger. Falken was not sure which. He often found her mood often difficult to read.

She asked the obvious question with an arched eyebrow. "Then why have you come?"

"I need to speak with Jade."

A flash of feminine jealousy furrowed her brow. "What about?"

"I need to question her about one of her clients."

The fire burned brighter. "Herbert, you know I can't allow that. Discretion and anonymity are the foundation of my business."

"You and your girls cooperated when we investigated Kingman."

"That was different. Two of my girls were dead, and I had a duty to protect the others." Sarah crossed her arms over her bosom. "Are any of my girls in danger now?"

Falken pulled out his cigar case. "I have no reason to believe so."

Sarah planted her hands on her hips and thrust out her chin. "Then you've no right to ask me to betray a gentleman's confidentiality, Herbert Falken. Your special privileges have limits. How would you feel if I permitted someone to come in here and ask questions about you or James?"

"The man is the prime suspect in the murder of Alderman Garrett."

"Herbert, you can't—"

"Mrs. Bannon, we believe the same man tried to kill the major just this morning," Westfall interjected.

Sarah's eyes went wide, and her mouth fell open. "My god. Are you hurt?"

Lighting his cigar, Falken shook his head. "The assassin missed his mark." Exhaling a cloud of smoke at the ceiling, he added, "And to be clear, we're not certain it was the same man."

With a pained expression, Sarah massaged her temples. "What happened?"

Falken briefly detailed the shooting.

"Damn you," Sarah said. "If you go and get yourself killed, I'll … I'll never forgive you for it. Go away, somewhere safe, until this maniac is caught."

Falken drew on his cigar. "Please, I need to speak with Jade."

Sarah paced a small circle, alternately glancing between Falken, the floor, and the ceiling. Her expression changed from shock and panic back to anger, then concern and sorrow. After a few minutes, shoulders sagging, eyes misty, she turned to Falken.

"I'll help you this time, because you're in danger, but don't ever ask this of me again." She crossed to the door, stopped, and said over her shoulder, "When you're finished, please leave. I can't talk to you anymore right now."

Several minutes later, Jade entered the parlor. Her hair was mussed, her eyes were wary, and she wore a thin, nearly transparent silk dressing gown. It was obvious she had nothing on underneath. "Sarah says you want to talk to me."

"Yes, please close the doors and sit down," Falken replied.

Jade closed the pocket doors and crossed to a brocaded wingback chair. "She says you're going to ask me about a john, and I'm to tell you whatever you want to know."

"I understand your ethical dilemma, but this is important."

Jade turned to Westfall and smiled, then replied to Falken. "Her house, her rules. But first I want to ask you a question."

Falken nodded.

"Why does everyone call you Major?"

"It was my rank in the army."

"But you're not in the army anymore."

"No, I was discharged."

"Discharged? What did you do wrong?"

"The word 'discharged' has a different meaning in military usage. It simply means I left the army."

"Why? Don't soldiers usually stay with the army until retirement?"

Falken drew deeply on his cigar. "I performed a distasteful yet necessary duty. Afterward, my superiors felt it best that I leave the service."

Jade let out a short laugh. "I perform distasteful yet necessary duties all the time, but no one tells me to quit being a whore. Of course, some of my duties are more pleasurable than others." She smiled at Westfall again. "Were you discharged from the army too?"

Westfall returned the smile, with journal and fountain pen in hand. "Yes, I fell from my horse and broke my left leg in four places. The doctors say I'm crippled for life and therefore am unfit for military service."

"I wouldn't worry too much." Jade winked. "The important parts still work just fine."

"Jade, do you know a man named Liam Devlin?" Falken said.

She turned back to Falken. "Yes, Liam is one of my regulars. Why are you asking about him?"

"Describe him, please."

Jade gave a detailed physical description. In general, it matched Morrissey's description, and that of the messenger boy.

"Do you know where we might find him?" Falken said.

"No, Liam doesn't talk about himself much. He insists that I do most of the talking."

"When was he here last?"

"Saturday night."

Falken's eyes narrowed, and he stroked his mustache. "This past Saturday night? He was here then?"

"Yes."

"What time did he arrive?"

"A little before ten, like always."

"When did he leave?"

"Just after sunrise, like always."

"You're sure he was here all night?"

She giggled. "Major, you two aren't the only ones with overnight privileges. Liam comes to see me every Saturday night. And he always stays until sunrise. He's noisy about getting dressed and wakes me up."

"Did he seem out of sorts this past Saturday?"

"No." Jade shook her head. "He was the same old Liam. What's this about?"

"Has he threatened you?"

"Threatened me? Why would he?"

"Jade, Devlin is a murder suspect. I believe he murdered Alderman Charles Garrett this past Saturday night, in St. Louis. Now please tell me the absolute truth. Was he really here? Or did he tell you to lie to anyone asking about him?"

Jade leaned forward. "Murder? Major, I swear on my mother's life, I don't know anything about a murder. Liam is a criminal, I know that much. I grew up in a Dublin tenement full of petty thieves, swindlers, and ne'er-do-wells. My own dad was a safecracker. But I'm telling you Liam was here, and he's never said a word about any murder."

"You understand the consequences of lying about this?"

Jade nodded. "I'd be putting my head in the noose. I've told you the truth."

"And you haven't seen Devlin since early Sunday morning? He hasn't sent you a message?"

"No. He only comes here on Saturdays, and there are no letters, notes, or telegrams in between."

Falken stroked his mustache and stared at the ceiling, ignoring the cigar.

He knew that Devlin always did his own killing. The blackmail scheme had dried up, and Garrett had surely told him that Decker had folded the smuggling operation. Therefore Devlin would have been aware the scheme was known to others. He had to know he was exposed. A smart man would count his profit and move onto something else. He wouldn't kill a dupe out of spite and make himself the primary suspect.

No, Devlin was not a fool; he was a calculating criminal motivated solely by personal gain.

Falken stubbed his smoldering cigar out in a crystal ashtray. "I believe you. Thank you for cooperating." He nodded to Westfall.

Jade sighed with relief, stood and went to the bar. She reached over, grabbed a bottle of gin, and took a long pull. Still clutching the bottle, she began sobbing.

"You'll let us know if Devlin shows up here?" Falken said. "Or if you learn of his whereabouts?"

Head down, Jade nodded.

Falken and Westfall left in silence.

CHAPTER SIXTEEN

With the sound of horseshoes clopping and carriage wheels clattering, the carriage bounced along the brick-paved streets while Falken's thoughts drifted.

At times he felt like a fraud. He had gained a few minutes of national notoriety for "assuming command, upon the death of his superior officer, and vanquishing a scourge of blood-thirsty border raiders." The published version of events blamed a band of banditos and renegade Apaches for a months-long campaign of murder and terror along the Rio Grande. While this was true, it was not the whole truth. Newspaper reports omitted two potentially scandalous facts: U.S. Army deserters had comprised one-third of the band's strength, and Colonel Nathaniel Hawkins, Cavalry, U.S. Army, had mobilized and led the murderous savages.

Afterward, to lessen the likelihood of inconvenient questions from curious brother officers, the generals decided Falken had to go. While he convalesced at Fort Riley, a medical board specifically convened to review his case, concluded that the rigors of battle and captivity had left him physically unfit for service. An addendum to the final report suggested "the possibility of future mental disability." It was unfortunate, they said, that a promising career had to end, but it was necessary for the good of the army.

For better or worse, Falken had been a soldier and so had complied with his orders: involuntary separation and public silence regarding Hawkins. However, his role in the cover-up of Hawkins' savagery was a bitter pill.

The carriage bounced onto Eads Bridge.

Westfall broke the silence. "Do you really believe Jade?"

Falken blinked away his troubling memories and drew a deep breath. "Yes."

"Could she be mistaken about the time Devlin arrived?"

"Possibly, but not enough to make him the killer. He arrived about ten. Jade could be off by a quarter of an hour, maybe half an hour, but even if she's off by a full hour and Devlin didn't show up until eleven, he still couldn't have killed Garrett. Miss Heinen said she left Garrett around midnight."

"What if Miss Heinein got the time wrong as well?"

The mention of Gretchen Heinen brought her face into Falken's mind. Anna quickly followed, and he felt himself suffocating. A thousand icy knives plunged into his heart and he struggled to calm himself.

After half a minute, Falken said, "Even if Miss Heinen's also off by an hour, Devlin couldn't have killed Garrett around eleven and walked into Sarah's at the same time."

"So, either Devlin is not our man, or someone's lying about what happened and when." Westfall removed his bowler and wiped sweat from his brow with the back of his hand. "But you're convinced both Jade and Gretchen Heinen are telling the truth, so where does that leave us?"

The carriage eased to a stop. Westfall leaned out the open window for a look. A few seconds later, he plopped back into his seat. "A line has formed. Police are looking into carriages."

"Whatever for?"

Westfall shrugged in reply.

Minutes later, the carriage rolled forward and stopped again. A police sergeant opened the curbside door and poked his head in. His ruddy face lit with recognition and relief.

"There you are, Major Falken. Captain Morrissey's looking for you."

Irritated by the stifling heat, and the uncertainty of his investigation and memories, Falken snapped, "And what, pray tell, does the good captain want?"

"I don't know, Major, but now that I've found you I have to follow orders and take you to him."

"Very well," Falken said. When the two men had exited the carriage and Falken had paid the driver, he turned to the sergeant. "Where to?"

The sergeant pointed to a nearby police carriage. "Hop Alley."

Falken stepped down from the police carriage at Ninth and Market Streets, in the heart of St. Louis' postage-stamp Chinatown, also known as Hop Alley. The enclave, just three blocks square, was home to a few hundred Chinese immigrants. The principal businesses were hand laundries, teashops, and restaurants.

A police lieutenant who had been at the riverbank on Sunday morning waved from an alleyway. "This way, Major."

Falken and Westfall followed the lieutenant into the alley. About halfway down, they turned and passed through a nondescript door. A red-shaded lantern hung above the lintel. Inside, they walked along a short corridor then descended a staircase to the basement. Falken recognized the sweet pungent scent of opium smoke.

The dimly lit limestone-walled basement was crowded with rows of narrow Chinese rope beds. Policemen had gathered several Chinese, who stood about expressionless with their eyes downcast. A few white men and a couple of women, too intoxicated to move, lay on the beds.

Morrissey's voice called out, "Over here, Major."

Falken and Westfall moved toward the sound of the voice.

"What do we have here?" Falken asked.

Morrissey held a hissing kerosene lantern over the bed in front of him. A thin, redheaded, bearded man with a jagged scar on his right cheek lay on the bed, completely still.

"Major, meet Liam Devlin."

Falken looked down. "Is he dead?"

"Yes, Herbert," came the familiar voice of Dr. Evans. "He's dead. I'd say he expired a few hours ago."

Falken looked down on the man's peaceful waxen features. "How certain are you of the time of death, Doctor?" He reached down and lifted Devlin's right hand; the ring finger was missing.

"My cursory examination is far from accurate, but I estimate that he died before nine this morning. Probably after six."

Falken turned to Morrissey. "So …"

"So it's still possible that he shot at you around seven-thirty, then ran down here, smoked a pipe, and died."

"What does the proprietor say?"

"Nothing I can understand. Either he doesn't speak English or pretends not to. But you speak the Chinaman's lingo, don't you?"

"A little Cantonese. Enough to get from place to place and feed myself."

"Well, that's more than the rest of us." Morrissey raised his voice and called out, "Lieutenant, drag the head chink over here."

Moments later a small Chinese of indeterminate age came forward, flanked by two large policemen. Falken addressed the man in heavily accented Cantonese. A tentative nod and greeting were offered in reply.

After two minutes of halting conversation, augmented with impromptu hand gestures, Falken turned to the captain.

"He says Devlin's been here since Monday afternoon. He showed up with five of his lieutenants, after they'd heard about Garrett's murder. Since then, they've been alternating between here, the restaurant on the first floor, and the brothel on the second. He says none of them have left the building."

"Uh-huh," Morrissey said. "We bagged the others. They're singing the same tune. They claim Devlin figured we'd finger him for Garrett and decided to hide out. But I don't believe it. This chink," he said, pointing at the Chinese, "did business with Devlin for who knows how long. He and the others are lying to save themselves."

Falken spoke to the man in Cantonese again.

The Chinese pointed down and said, "Dead. No scare dead man. No lie."

"I still don't believe it," Morrissey said.

"I need to speak with you, Captain," Falken said, "in private."

"Why, Major? We've got our man."

"No, we have not."

"Because this chink says so?"

"I have corroboration."

Morrissey's face appeared shadowy in the lantern light, yet his sneer was unmistakable. "What?"

Falken sighed. "I spoke with Devlin's green-eyed beauty. Her name is Jade, and she works at Mrs. Bannon's. She swears Devlin was there from ten o'clock Saturday night until about six-thirty Sunday morning."

"And you're going to take the word of a whore?"

"Yes. I threatened to charge her as an accomplice, and she understands the consequences of lying to me."

"Why are you doing this?"

"The better question is why are *you* doing this, Captain?" Dr. Evans said. "If this Devlin didn't kill Charles, the actual murderer is still at large. Charles was a friend and I for one want to see justice done."

Morrissey motioned his men to move back out of hearing and spoke in a low tone. "City Hall wants an arrest. The chief wants an arrest. The well-to-do citizens of this city want an arrest. Hell, I'm told the governor is demanding an arrest be made forthwith, or he's going to order the police board to clean house. I'm up against the wall on this one."

"That's a poor excuse for ignoring the very real possibility that a murderer may still be roaming free," Evans said. "I know the governor; we served together in the army. If necessary, I'll go to Jefferson City and expose the sham you're proposing."

"Jesus, Mary and Joseph." Morrissey ran a hand over his face and locked eyes with Falken. "Very well, Major, who's next on the suspect list?"

"I don't have an alternate suspect yet."

"Well, you think about it," Morrissey said. Then he sneered at Evans and strode away.

No one spoke or moved.

After a full minute, Westfall broke the silence. "Major, if Devlin didn't try to kill you this morning, who did?"

"Who indeed?"

CHAPTER SEVENTEEN

As early evening shadows lengthened, Falken sat in his library with Westfall and Owen; Mrs. Howard had gone home for the evening. His jacket and vest were off, his loosened necktie hung below an unbuttoned collar, and his shirtsleeves were rolled up to the elbow. His cigar case and Merwin Hulbert Pocket Army revolver, chambered for the .44-40 Winchester, lay on the reading table next to a nearly empty, sweating tea glass. A small-frame .32 was concealed in his jacket.

Westfall had spent the previous two hours reading his case notes aloud from the beginning. Per orders, his Colt New Army Model 1896 revolver rode on his right hip in an army-issue holster, suspended from an issue pistol belt.

Owen sat on a chair by the open door, his Mauser Broomhandle pistol secured in the shoulder holster, and a Winchester Model 97 shotgun against the wall, inches away. He seemed to be making a conscious effort to keep himself between his officers and the front door.

Falken pinched the bridge of his nose. "What have we missed? Who have we overlooked? Owen, you're hearing all of this for the first time. Does anything stand out to you?"

"Well, it seems clear that Mr. Decker had reason to wish harm on Alderman Garrett."

"True, Decker has a wagonload of motive, but no opportunity."

"Unless he had an accomplice," added Westfall.

Falken nodded. "Noted." He looked up. "Anyone else, Owen?"

"Mr. Vesper made a good point. There are a lot of men who've lost jobs and are owed money, and they're not likely to be mourning Garrett."

"Again, true. But anger is a long way from murderous rage. Keep in mind that Garrett was stabbed and savagely beaten. The beating indicates a personal motive, something above and beyond money."

"I'm not so sure—"

The telephone ringing in the hallway interrupted Owen. The orderly rose, picked up the shotgun, and stepped into the hallway. A few seconds later he returned and said, "Major, a Mr. Adams is calling."

Falken picked up his large revolver and went to the telephone. "Adams?"

The line crackled and popped. "Major, it's just terrible, sir. I can't believe it."

"Can't believe what, Adams?"

"Gretchen. The police were just here. Gretchen has been arrested for Charles's murder."

Damn that man, thought Falken. He was going to arrest someone, *anyone*, and to hell with the truth. "Who made the arrest? Captain Morrissey?"

"Yes, the captain who came to the house with you and Dr. Evans."

"Did he say where she was taken?"

"Police headquarters for interrogation. I won't argue with anyone who says she's a tramp, but a murderess? I can't accept that anyone in this house would harm Charles."

"All right, I'll do what I can." Falken hung up the receiver. After taking a moment to calm himself, he strode back into the library, rolling down his shirtsleeves. "I'm going downtown."

"I overheard," Westfall said. "Morrissey really arrested the maid?"

"Yes."

"He didn't waste any time finding a new suspect." Westfall packed up the satchel. "I'll go with you."

Falken nodded and continued to dress. "Owen, you too. I don't like the idea of leaving you here alone."

The young man grinned. "It'll take me just a minute to get ready." He left the library.

"What's Morrissey playing at?" said Westfall.

"You heard him this afternoon. Everyone wants an arrest. Guilt or innocence doesn't seem to matter at this point."

With the last rays of twilight on the western horizon, Falken and company stepped off the trolley at Market and Twelfth Streets, a block from the Four Courts Building that housed police headquarters, the city jail, criminal courts, police courts, and related offices. With whistles sounding and locomotives chugging in and out of Union Station half a dozen blocks to the west, they marched south toward Clark Avenue. The evening air was cool, yet still thick with humidity and soot.

Falken had always thought the Four Courts—a three-story, block-long cream sandstone structure with a squared cupola on each end, and a large, square central dome—resembled a small fortress. He also thought that was the exact impression a building representing law and order ought to convey: strength, impregnability and permanence.

The trio passed street sweepers using brooms and shovels to clean up piles of horse manure along Clark Avenue and entered the Four Courts. A few foot patrolmen dragged or prodded prisoners toward the building, while others headed back out to their assigned areas. A mounted patrolman stood at each end of the block, watching for trouble. A barking dog chased a cat into a nearby alley.

The three men crossed the broad lobby beneath the dome, and took a wide public staircase to the second floor. The architecture and craftsmanship were of the modified Renaissance style common to many public buildings; it was functional, yet grand. Sweepers and floor polishers were just beginning their evening's work, along with window washers and other janitorial staff.

On the second-floor landing, an immaculately turned out lieutenant looked up from behind a reception desk. "May I help you, gentlemen?"

Westfall stepped forward. "Major Falken to see Captain Morrissey."

The lieutenant looked Falken up and down, frowned and picked up the telephone receiver. To the switchboard operator, he said, "Captain Morrissey." A minute later, he spoke again. "Lieutenant Ballard, reception. There's a Major Falken and two other men here." He listened, then replied, "Yes, Captain."

After hanging up the receiver, the lieutenant said, "The captain says you can join him. Do you know where interrogation is?"

"Yes," Falken said, and the three marched, in step, down the corridor.

Owen observed, sotto voce, "He doesn't like you, Major."

"As shocking as it might seem, there are those who do not revere our efforts on behalf of the citizenry. Some particularly ambitious mid-level policemen look upon us as unwelcome interlopers or annoying amateurs."

Owen shrugged.

They turned down a side corridor and found Captain Morrissey waiting outside a closed door. A carved wooden sign on the door read: *Interrogation Room No. 2.*

Eyes blazing, Falken opened his mouth to speak, but Morrissey held up his right hand, palm out. "Just simmer down, Major, I've been expecting you. The butler was on the telephone before I even got her out the door." He crossed his arms and held his chin with his left hand. "I told you I was going to question her after Devlin was found, so here we are."

"Has Miss Heinen made a spontaneous confession?"

"No, I've been waiting for you. I don't want any doubt in your mind about what happens here, so that you can proceed with a clear conscience and assure Dr. Evans. The last thing I need or want is the doctor talking to the governor about this case. I'm getting an earful from the chief, and City Hall, morning, noon and night. I don't need anyone else telling me how to do my job."

With a grim expression, Falken nodded. Politics. He knew that in the end, every ugly job was spawned, in some manner, by politics. Several uniformed faces flashed before his mind's eye, along with the countenance of Colonel Nathaniel Hawkins. The memories caused an icy flutter deep in his belly.

Morrissey opened the door and motioned the trio inside. He walked in behind Owen, closed the door, and took a chair on the near side of a stout oak table. The table's legs were bolted to the floor. The rough-hewn tabletop bore dark stains, possibly blood, that had soaked into the wood.

Falken motioned his staff into a pair of chairs along the left-hand wall. A middle-aged patrolman sat behind a small writing desk against the opposite wall, ready to transcribe the interrogation. The captain had not provided a third observer's chair, obviously not expecting Owen's presence.

While Westfall prepared to take his own notes, Falken stared at Gretchen Heinen amid fleeting mental images of Anna. The resemblance seemed to be more pronounced each time he laid eyes on her. The waves of her hair, her dainty cheekbones and chin, slender nose, long thin fingers, even the size and shape of her bosom; all seemed to be an exact copy of his lost love. His heart ached.

Gretchen sat on a chair opposite Morrissey. She tried to hide her hands on her lap. Iron manacles, attached to heavy chains bolted to the floor, were locked around her wrists. Her head was bowed and her face was flushed, and there was a trace of wetness on her cheeks. She did not move; she barely seemed to breathe.

The sight of her, in her humiliation, was almost more than Falken could bear. *You poor, beautiful, innocent child. Don't worry, I'll clear your name and set things right. You have my word. I won't allow anyone to harm you or sully your name further. No matter what it takes, I'll find the murderer and set you free. Then—*

Morrissey cleared his throat and shuffled through a sheaf of papers laid out on the table. "Major Falken," he said to Gretchen, nodding to his left, "provided me with a transcript of his interrogation of you yesterday afternoon. I'd like to revisit a point or two with you now."

Gretchen slowly raised her head, blinked tear-filled eyes, and nodded.

"You confessed that you seduced Charles Garrett, and that you were his mistress."

Another nod. *"Ja."*

"You also confessed that he proposed to leave his family, and that he promised to take you to San Francisco."

"Ja."

"Did he promise you a life of wealth and privilege?"

"He said I would want for nothing."

"Did he intend to marry you?"

"Yes, he loved me, and I loved him."

"Are you pregnant with the illegitimate child of Charles Garrett?"

Fresh tears ran down Gretchen's cheeks. "Must you be so crude?"

"We are talking about a child conceived outside marriage, who will be born to an unwed mother. Would you prefer the word *bastard*?"

Gretchen tried to rise, but the rattling chains stopped her. Dropping back onto the chair, she said, "It takes one to know one."

Morrissey looked up from the transcript. "Are you pregnant with Charles Garrett's bastard child?"

Eyes still burning with contempt, she spat out, "Yes."

"Have you also stated that upon learning of your pregnancy, Garrett rejected you and the unborn child?"

"He was shocked. Given time, he would have taken it back. He loved me." Gretchen glanced at Falken, as if seeking his support.

"So do you confirm that he rejected you and the child?"

"I confirm that he was shocked and angry."

"You also confessed you were angry. So angry that you attacked him with a baseball bat."

"I was afraid! I thought he was going to kill me."

"But you say he loved you. He loved you, yet he ordered you out of his life. He loved you, yet he rejected your child. He loved you, yet he threatened to harm you. You loved him, but you feared for your life. You loved him, but you struck two potentially lethal blows. Do you see the contradictions?"

"I see you trying to twist my words. Why aren't you trying to find Charles's killer instead of harassing me?"

"But I have found his murderer." Morrissey stood and leaned across the table. "You've confessed more than enough motive to convince a jury. Hell hath no fury like a spurned mistress." He thrust a finger under Gretchen's nose. She drew back and turned her head away. "You've also admitted to attacking him with a bat on the very night he died. In fact, you told Major Falken you feared you'd killed him."

"I did not!"

"Oh, but you did." Morrissey searched through the papers and found the passage he was looking for. "I quote, 'I know I injured his head, but I swear he was alive when I ran out. Did I kill him?' Do you now deny making this statement? Are you accusing Major Falken and Mr. Westfall of conspiring against you?"

"You're twisting my words again."

"The only thing being twisted here is the truth, by you. I've established motive and opportunity. Finish your confession.

The only parts you've left out are the stabbing, moving the corpse, and dumping it in the river. I promise you'll feel much better after you tell us the whole truth."

Gretchen shook her head and began sobbing. "No, I didn't. I didn't do it." Her shoulders and arms trembled.

Morrissey slapped his palm on the table, making Gretchen and Owen jump. "Name your accomplice. Who helped you load him in the wagon? Who drove the body to the riverbank?" He slapped the table again. "Confess! Who stole Garrett's belongings? Who dumped him in the Mississippi?" Another hard, loud slap. "Who are you protecting?"

"I didn't do *anything*. I didn't kill Charles. I loved him." Gretchen's head was bowed. She continued trembling and sobbing, and her lips moved, speaking unintelligible words.

"Given your pregnancy, if that too is not a lie I'm confident the prosecuting attorney will recommend leniency. If you make a full confession, identify your accomplice, and testify against him, you'll be tried by a jury of twelve honest men, convicted, and, after the birth of your child, taken to the gallows."

Morrissey leaned across the table again. "Have you seen a hanging?" He let the question hang in the air for a moment. "You'll be standing over the trapdoor with a hood covering your head, and your arms and legs bound with heavy leather straps. You'll hear footsteps, and sense someone standing near. Then the deputy warden will slide the noose over your head and pull it tight. Can you feel it?" Another dramatic pause. "A clergyman will read a passage from the Bible, something about redemption. Then the warden will read your death warrant. The whole time you'll be standing there, knowing what's coming, waiting for it. Finally you'll hear a clunk as the executioner pulls the lever. You'll feel yourself falling into the pit of hell. When you hit the end of the rope, the last sound you'll hear is your own neck snapping."

Gretchen continued to sob and quiver, but remained silent.

Morrissey stood erect, glanced to his left and nodded toward the door. "Confession is your only path to salvation. I'll give you some time to think about the consequences of your actions, and the last minutes of your life." He went to the door and opened it.

With ice flowing through his veins and pounding in his ears, and his mind burning with rage, Falken rose and followed Morrissey out of the room. Westfall and Owen were right behind him.

When Morrissey closed the door, Falken spoke, his words dripping venom. "What kind of man are you? Did you enjoy that charade?"

"Major, I'm just doing my job. It's unpleasant at times, but it's necessary. You ought to understand that."

"*Unpleasant?* Now there's an understatement. Verbally torturing a distraught child, threatening her with hang—"

"I can't believe you don't see it. We have more evidence against her than we had on Devlin. You were perfectly willing to condemn him with circumstantial innuendo. She's voluntarily incriminated herself." Morrissey scratched his head. "Has this girl bewitched you?"

Falken stabbed an accusing finger across the space between them. "Every statement you threw at her was taken out of context. You were twisting words, and trying to confuse and trick a scared girl. Make an arrest, any arrest will do. Put someone, *anyone*, in jail to placate the politicians." He deflated and spat out, "It makes me sick."

Morrissey turned to Westfall. "You were present for both interrogations. She incriminated herself by admitting motive and opportunity. Do you believe her denials, or the facts at hand?"

Westfall glanced at Falken, then met Morrissey's gaze. With steel in his voice, he said, "I have every confidence in Major Falken's investigative abilities. He understands the criminal mind in ways I can't fathom. If he can look into a dark soul and identify the evil within, he can do the same with an innocent. If he believes her, then so do I."

To Falken, Morrissey said, "I told you I want no doubt in your mind. Question her again, if you wish. Give her an alibi, if you can.

Provide me with another likely suspect, and I'll pursue him like the hounds of hell. Until then, I'm duty bound to go where the facts lead me."

Falken calmed himself and said, "I would like to question her again."

With a smirk, Morrissey extended his arm toward the door.

They reentered the room. Westfall and Owen reclaimed their seats, and Falken and Captain Morrissey remained standing.

Falken stroked his mustache and said, "Miss Heinen, I asked you if Garrett was afraid of anyone, and you said no. Can you think of anyone who wanted to harm him? Did anyone have a grudge against him? Did he mention any threats or confrontations?"

Gretchen looked up with red-rimmed eyes. She leaned forward. Her voice was low, tentative. "Charles didn't like the bookkeeper, Keller. He wasn't specific, but I could tell there was mistrust." She thought for several moments, then added, "I remember thinking he might have been blackmailing Charles."

"What made you think that?"

"There was something, things he said. He railed about his money problems, but he never went into detail. I can't explain it, but I remember considering the possibility."

"Does anyone else come to mind?"

"The steamboat man, Decker, was very angry with Charles. Charles also mentioned a man in Chicago, a gambler. He said the man accused him of cheating and threatened to take revenge. But he never gave me his name."

"When was this?"

"Last spring, April, I think." Gretchen paused and sniffed loudly. "Charles went to Chicago on business."

"Does Keller know about the room?"

"Everyone at the House knows. Keller certainly. Charles told me he accounted for the furnishings and plumbing as a private office. He paid for it with company money."

"Thank you." Falken looked to Morrissey.

Morrissey said, "That'll be it, for now." To the patrolman seated at the writing desk, he said, "Call the matron to take her away, then type that transcription."

Falken looked at Gretchen; her pleading expression cut him deep. If any man had ever treated Anna so—

"We're finished here, Major," Morrissey said.

Falken tore his eyes away and exited the room.

In the corridor, Westfall said, "It's strange that Keller didn't mention the special room."

"I'll grant you it's strange," replied Morrissey, "but his omission could be nothing more than subordinate loyalty, shielding the reputation of his employer from scandal."

With a faraway expression, Falken said, "We'll know more after speaking with him again."

"We may or may not. Either way, it'll keep until tomorrow," Morrissey said.

"Tomorrow? We do nothing, while she spends the night in a stinking jail cell?"

"Major, it's been a long day, yet another long day. I'm going home to my supper, a few bottles of beer, and my bed. I suggest you do the same. I'll send a carriage for you in the morning."

Falken started to protest again, but stopped himself. Like it or not, the girl's fate rested in Morrissey's hands. Continuing to antagonize the man would do little to help her. "Very well, we shall continue in the morning."

CHAPTER EIGHTEEN

It seemed to go on for hours. *His mother's sobbing pleading voice, clearly heard through thin walls. No! You promised. You promised not to do* this again. You promised.

He cowered beneath the heavy quilt while her shrieks of pain and fear stabbed his heart. He desperately wanted to go to her aid, to end the suffering, to save her, to give her vengeance, but every horrible sound redoubled his own fright—a yelp, whiskey-laced grunts and curses, a dull thud, footfalls, another yelp, something fragile crashing to the floor. He was paralyzed and hated himself as only a coward could.

As her wails of anguish continued, he shivered and recited the mantra: "When I'm big and strong, I will fight him. When I'm big and strong, I will fight him. When—"

The tone of her voice had suddenly changed. Now it was … angry … defiant … determined … Then she howled. Something else crashed.

He heard roaring, cursing.

There was a flurry of noise. She cried, "Herbert!" Then nothing.

The house was silent. There were no more voices, no cries or pleas, no grunts or taunts, no breaking of glassware or crockery, no creaking and muffled moans from their bedroom. Utter inexplicable silence.

After an eternity of wide-eyed, open-mouthed, heart-pounding listening, he heard a rush of heavy footfalls. Then the front door slammed.

He shivered; the air went right through his clothing, prickling his skin. Small snowflakes fell from lead-gray clouds; an inch or so covered the ground.

A couple dozen people stood with heads bowed: his aunt, uncle, cousins and women from the parish. His aunt held his left hand, and his uncle stood behind with strong hands resting on his shoulders. Flanked by a pair of altar boys, Father Hembrow recited a prayer in Latin. The words were familiar, yet incomprehensible to a thirteen-year-old boy.

His mother's coffin rested on boards over the open grave. Two thick ropes were laid out for lowering the plain pine box into the hole.

His eyes darted around the cemetery, searching fearfully for his stepfather. His uncle's assurances that Adolph Tuchman had run away rang hollow. Tuchman was evil. Father Hembrow had always said, "Be vigilant, boys. Evil can spring from any quarter without warning."

As the prayer droned on, he asked God why his mother had to die. Was it a punishment? Was she bad? Had he been bad? Over the years, he had asked God the same questions about his real father. He stood shivering in the cold, waiting for answers.

Anna was smiling and laughing. She collided with the railing; her expression changed to surprise; then her face showed shock, fear and helplessness in rapid succession as momentum carried her backward over the side.

"Noooooo!"

Leaning over, he watched her fall through the air, arms and legs flailing. He thought she mouthed, I love you. *Then her body landed on the riverbank. He was sure he heard her bones crack and snap. She lay facedown, motionless, with her head and upper body in the water.*

He was struck by the thought that she might have survived the fall and was simply unconscious. Perhaps she was drowning at that very moment. Running with fear-fueled energy, he reached the end of the bridge, waved at a nearby policeman, pointed toward the river, and charged headlong down the levee.

A slow-moving southbound train blocked his path for several excruciating minutes.

Anna! Anna, please don't die. I'm coming to help you.

Two patrolmen arrived, and while they waited for the train to pass he frantically explained. Finally the train cleared and he darted across the tracks.

At the riverbank, they pulled Anna out of the water; her body was a sack of broken bones, and her beautiful skin had already turned ash-gray. He felt for a pulse, begged the patrolmen for help, pleaded to God. Why? Why is my Anna dead? What have I done to deserve this? Am I being punished?

No reply came down from the heavens.

He stood on the bridge, looking out over the river. A heavy fog obscured the water. Distant steamboats blew whistles; a church bell tolled; a pack of dogs barked and growled.

He called out, "Anna, where are you? I can't see you."

Seconds, minutes, hours may have passed; he had no sense of time. "Anna, don't taunt me by hiding in the fog. I must see you. I need you. I love you."

With a swirl, the mist parted and Anna stood in the river. However, she did not speak, nor look at him. Instead, she stared at the spot where she had died.

"Anna, my love, why will you not speak to me? I am here. Please look at me."

Anna continued to stare in silence.

The paralyzing fear gripped his insides, held his head, numbed his arms and legs. Eyes squeezed shut, he said, "I will not look at that awful spot. Please don't torment me. I only want to hear your voice. I only want to hear your lovely sweet voice."

"Herbert."

Eyes tightly closed, his ears picked up the sound of a voice he had not heard in so very long. Was this some trick? Was the strange fog distorting sound?

"Herbert, open your eyes."

He opened his eyes and burst into tears. His mother stood in the river next to Anna.

"Herbert, you must swallow your fear and do your best. I've never asked more than that of you."

"Mother, I'm sorry. I'm so sorry. I wanted to help you, but I was scared. He was too big—"

"Do as she asks, Herbert. Swallow your fear and do as she asks."

"Yes, Mother." He steeled himself for the horror and looked to the riverbank. The fog parted, and he saw Garrett laying half in and half out of the water.

"You know what happened."

He looked straight ahead again. His mother was gone, but Anna met his gaze. "You know what happened."

"Anna, my Love. Mother, where are you? Come back."

The mist closed in and Anna faded from view.

"No! Anna, come back to me. Please come back. Anna!"

Falken snapped awake, lunging upward into the darkness. Bathed in sweat, his heart hammered, and his lungs heaved. With another desperate cry on his lips, he let his arms fall and he collapsed back onto the pillow. Tears flowed freely as he stared up at the bed canopy.

Surely I'm being punished by a vengeful God, he thought. Is it for my cowardice? For my foolish negligence? For leading my men to their slaughter? When will my penance be complete?

After long minutes of self-recrimination, he wiped his eyes with the bedsheet. Then he sat up and got out of bed. His watch, barely visible in the dark, read three-thirty.

He listened for several moments. Satisfied he hadn't disturbed Westfall, Falken slipped on his house shoes and crept to the tower. Though he craved peaceful oblivion, he also needed to think. He needed answers.

CHAPTER NINETEEN

The police carriage braked to a stop on Market Street in front of Garrett House. Captain Morrissey was standing at the bottom of the steps with a sergeant and a patrolman.

Falken and Westfall stepped down. Owen had been left behind to guard the house and Mrs. Howard.

Shaking his head, Morrissey said, "Keller's not here. Actually, there's very few inside, underlings mostly. Probably pilfering whatever the higher-ups haven't carted off."

"Did you search his office?" Falken said.

"No, but you're welcome to have a look."

Falken bounded up the steps and rushed inside. The reception desk was unmanned. He marched to the elevator, also unattended, and saw an out-of-order sign hanging from the accordion gate. Spinning around, he saw Morrissey and Westfall waiting by the stairway door.

Falken ignored the captain's you're-wasting-your-time expression and took the stairs two at a time. Winded, he arrived at Keller's office door on the third floor and twisted the knob. Locked. Damn.

Westfall and Morrissey walked into the corridor.

"I presume you already knew it was locked," Falken said to Morrissey.

Morrissey nodded with a smirk.

"May I?" Falken said, indicating the door.

Morrissey turned away, hands clasped behind his back.

Falken took a step back and kicked the door just below the knob. Wood creaked, but the door held. With a stinging foot, he kicked again and again. At last the jamb broke with a loud crack, and the door swung inward.

Falken pushed through the doorway and methodically swept his eyes over the wardrobe-sized office. The desk was neatly organized with stacks of invoices and other documents. A typewriter sat on a side table in the far corner, adjacent to the desk. Shelves above held paper, ribbons, and other clerical supplies. There was a squat iron safe in a corner, in front of the desk.

Falken went to the safe and tugged open the black-painted door. He quickly rifled the contents, discovering nothing but leather-bound ledgers and journals. It occurred to him that Keller, in a display of Teutonic efficiency, had probably left the safe unlocked for bank examiners and litigating attorneys, who would need to sift through the bankrupt firm's financials.

He moved around the desk, sat on the chair, and opened every drawer. He found nothing but fountain pens, pencils, and other items of the accounting clerk's trade.

Standing in the doorway, Morrissey said, "She's got you chasing your tail. Pitching Keller to us is nothing more than a ploy to muddy the water."

"I can't accept that. She's nineteen, for god's sake, a child. What does she know about conspiracy and murder?"

"Major, I could show you children who know plenty about it. The innocence of youth is a thing of the past."

Falken glared in reply.

"What's this hold she seems to have over you? Are you forgetting she seduced her married employer and had designs on taking him away from his own children?"

Stroking his mustache, Falken ignored the questions and concentrated on his thoughts. A moment later, he pulled out his wallet and withdrew a card. "I have Keller's address, 1577 North 18th Street, apartment five. I had him write it down when we were here."

"The man's probably out looking for a new job, but I'll go along."

"She's innocent, and I'll prove it."

The police carriage stopped in front of Keller's apartment building. Like the rest of the block, the two-story brick structure had been erected shortly after the Civil War and was beginning to show its age. From one end of the block to the other, every window was open; some curtained, others not. Laundry hung on clotheslines stretched across the narrow alleyways. Children played in the street. Several mothers, taking a break from their morning chores, sat on steps or leaned out windows, talking; most stared at the intruders, while others pretended not to notice them.

The driver remained with the horses and carriage while the others went inside, Falken leading the way.

Apartment five was on the second floor, left rear. A patrolman remained at the bottom of the stairs and the sergeant took his post at the top; both were tasked with keeping the curious at bay.

Falken knocked on Keller's door.

The door across the hallway opened and a frumpy, middle-aged woman peered out.

"Nothing to see here, ma'am," said the sergeant.

The matronly busybody took her time studying the strangers.

The sergeant cleared his throat. "Please go back inside, ma'am."

She waved a dismissive, wrinkled hand at the policeman. "You don't scare me, flatfoot." Then she closed the door sharply.

Falken knocked again.

Moments later, the lock turned and the door opened a crack. Eyes appeared, then the door opened fully. Franz Keller, dressed in brown trousers with matching vest and necktie, glanced at Falken, Westfall and Morrissey. "May I help you?"

"Mr. Keller, I'm Herbert Falken. We spoke at your office the day before yesterday."

"Yes, I remember, Herr Falken. How may I help you?"

"I need to ask you a few more questions."

Keller glanced over his shoulder. "Now is not a good time. I'm in a bit of a rush. Perhaps next week."

"I apologize for the inconvenience, but I need just a few minutes of your time."

"I'm sorry, I can't be delayed." Keller swung the door to close it.

Falken put his shoulder to the door and heaved, knocking the smaller Keller backward. Then he crossed the threshold and said, "I really must insist."

Taken aback, Keller said, "What is the meaning of this? You've no right to force your way into my home."

"As I said, just a few more questions. We're trying to bring your employer's murderer to justice."

Morrissey stepped into the three-room apartment. He spotted a large trunk, two leather suitcases, and a leather satchel on the floor next to a threadbare armchair. "Going somewhere?"

Keller glanced at his luggage. "Yes … yes, I'm going to Milwaukee. My sister and her husband live there. I may be able to secure employment with the Pabst Brewing Company. If I'm delayed, I'll miss my train."

Morrissey's eyes narrowed. "If you're moving to Milwaukee today, how could you be here next week to answer Major Falken's questions?"

"I'll only be gone a few days, a week at most. I must go and make inquiries before committing to a course of action."

Falken said, "That's a lot of luggage for a man who only plans to be gone a few days."

"I'm thinking the same thing," Morrissey added. "You better come with us." He jerked his head toward the door. "You can always take a train to Milwaukee tomorrow. I'm sure your sister and Mr. Pabst will understand."

Keller glanced at his luggage again, and nodded.

CHAPTER TWENTY

The windowless room was warm, the air close. Keller sat in the suspect's chair, in interrogation room two, but was not manacled. Falken was seated across the table. Morrissey stood by the door. Westfall occupied the writing desk, ready to take notes; none saw the need for two transcriptions.

Falken took his time preparing and lighting a cigar. While doing so, he held eye contact with Keller. The unimposing bookkeeper frowned and fidgeted, but did not look away; his eyes were clouded over and hard to read.

Wreathed in a cloud of smoke, Falken mentally counted off two minutes. The room was silent, save for a pair of flies buzzing from wall to wall. When he reached one hundred and ten, Keller looked away, his face betraying a hint of concern.

After another deep draw on his cigar, Falken began. "You're a fastidious man. Your trade requires accuracy and attention to the smallest of details. You even thought to leave your safe unlocked for those who might need access to Garrett's ledgers in your absence." He drew on the cigar. "Therefore I find it strange that you failed to mention Garrett's private room at the back of Garrett House. Can you explain that?"

Keller squirmed in the chair. "As you say, it was Herr Garrett's private room. What he used it for was none of my concern."

"I didn't ask if you know what went on within those walls. I asked why you didn't tell us about its existence."

Keller sighed. "I was being loyal and thought it my duty to protect Herr Garrett's dignity."

"Was he doing something undignified? You claim to be ignorant of the room's purpose."

"Herr Garrett's private affairs were not my concern. That's not to say I was unaware. I did my job and pretended not to notice. Discretion is a part of loyalty."

"But certainly a man of your intellect understands the importance of examining a murder victim's private, in this case secret, space?"

"Accounting is my trade. I leave crime solving to the police."

Falken puffed on the cigar again and stroked his mustache. "He died in that room. Was murdered there. Of course you know that, and that's why you kept the secret. Your guilty mind prevented you from revealing the murder scene to the police. You were protecting yourself, not your employer."

"You accuse me? Outrageous."

"You're intimately familiar with the details of the blackmail scheme. You're the only one Garrett confided in. You knew the company was failing and that you would soon be unemployed. You said you met with Liam Devlin several times. How much did he pay you for doing it? Enough to relocate to Milwaukee and start a new life?"

"What a fantastic tale. Why don't you ask Herr Devlin why he committed murder? He's the criminal, not I."

"I can't question Devlin because he's dead. Even so, I discovered exculpatory evidence that proves Garrett did not die by his hand. Your plan to shift the blame to a notorious criminal has failed."

Keller's eyes clouded over again. Then he said, "I have no plan."

"Do you know who Garrett's mistress was?"

"No."

"She told us everyone at Garrett House knew. Did you never hear any loose talk?"

"I'm not a gossip, and I don't abide those who are."

"What made you change your plan?"

"I have no plan."

"Not have, *had*. Past tense." Falken stroked his mustache again. "Allow me to refresh your memory. You stood in the alleyway in shadow, or possibly in the wagonhouse, waiting. You watched the girl run across the alleyway. When she walked away from the wagonhouse minutes later, you continued to wait, making certain she did not return. Then you crept through the open door. Garrett saw you, asked what you were doing there. You approached him on some pretense, possibly feigned concern over the open door. The knife was in your hand, held behind your leg out of his sight."

"When you were close"—Falken stood up and leaned across the table—"*this* close, you struck." He thrust his cigar at Keller's chest. "You stabbed him. He reeled away and you pursued, continuing to thrust the blade into him. He fell onto the bed, and you leapt on top of him. Thirteen times you stabbed him. But Garrett was a large, strong man."

With his face just inches from Keller's, Falken said, "In a desperate attempt to escape, he sat up and pushed you away." Falken withdrew to his side of the table and sat down. "He tried to regain his feet, but collapsed facedown across the foot of the bed. You watched while the blood drained out of him onto the mattress. You stood and callously watched as the life of another human being slipped away. When you were sure he would move no more, you rolled him onto the floor. Realizing you were liberally covered with the dead man's blood, you went to the basin and washed your hands and face."

Falken stood and paced the width of the small room, puffing on his cigar. "Then you went outside and pulled the movable steps clear of the door. You crossed to the wagonhouse. Garrett had ordered you to make keys to the security chain's padlock for Devlin's gang. You kept one for yourself, and used it to free the chain across the bay door. You have soft clerk's hands and are unaccustomed to working with animals, so it took time for you to hitch a team to a wagon by yourself. Darkness multiplied the difficulty of your task, but once you had it right, you led the horses into the alleyway, positioned the wagon alongside the open door, and removed the side panel. Next came the hard part. Garrett was twice your size. How were you going to move that much dead weight across the room and onto the wagon?"

Falken turned to Keller. "You took the top sheet from the bed and spread it out next to the body," he said, mimicking the action. "Then you knelt down and rolled him over. With a wad of bedsheet in each hand, you grunted and cussed and pulled his bulk across the room, inches at a time. Your back protested every tug. Your arms and legs burned from the effort. Your backside was sore because you fell several times. But you finally had him loaded. With the wagon out of the way and the steps back in place, you tidied up and took his coat from a peg on the wall to conceal your own bloody clothing."

Falken shook his finger at the ceiling. "At the last minute, it occurred to you that leaving the door unlocked was a bad idea. Someone might incidentally discover the scene of the crime before you were fully prepared. So you searched Garrett's pockets looking for his keys. You found the keyring, but only after emptying every other pocket. There was no time to return his possessions to his person. My god, you'd been exposed to public view for what must have seemed an eternity. Every passing second increased the threat of discovery. So you stuffed his things into your own pockets and were off."

Keller sat mutely, eyes downcast.

"The temptation to panic and drive the horses hard and fast through the city must have been excruciating," Falken said. "You knew someone somewhere had eyes on you, and those eyes saw Garrett's corpse bouncing along on the wagonbed. But you tamed your fears and remained calm. You drove along, slow and easy, just another teamster doing his night's work. You bumped onto the bridge. I think you were going to cross over to East St. Louis and dump the corpse in a Negro neighborhood. Certainly questions would have been asked. But in the end everyone would have accepted the murder and robbery of a wealthy white man by black-skinned hoodlums as one of life's unfortunate tragedies."

Falken drew on the cigar and thoughtfully exhaled a cloud of smoke. "However, you changed your plan. You drove onto the bridge and pulled over to the right-hand railing. After looking ahead and behind for any sign of a witness, you removed the side panel and rolled Garrett over the side."

Standing to Keller's right and looking down on him, Falken said, "The corpse has a number of broken bones. At first we assumed Garrett had been on the receiving end of a savage beating. We further assumed said beating had occurred before he was stabbed to death." He shook his finger at the ceiling again. "But the more I think about it, the more I'm convinced this version of events simply doesn't fit the facts. Given Garrett's size and temperament, a man of your small stature could not have beaten him hard enough and long enough to shatter so many bones without retaliation. So it was not a deliberate act. His body was broken when it landed on the riverbank."

Casually puffing on his cigar while walking around the table to once again face Keller, Falken crossed his arms and locked eyes with the accused. "I know what you did and how you did it. But I don't know why you dropped him off the bridge."

Keller was sweating freely, but his gaze remained steady, almost icy. "Herr Falken, you're a talented storyteller with a vivid imagination. But I don't know what you're talking about."

Keller's demeanor and a mental image of Gretchen behind bars caused Falken to lose his temper. "Damn you, man. Have you no decency? An innocent girl stands accused of your crime."

Keller's hard gaze melted in an instant. "Wh-what girl?"

"Garrett's mistress, Gretchen Heinen."

Keller turned to Morrissey. "Will you arrest her?"

"Already have," the captain said. "She's in the women's lockup and will be charged with murder tomorrow morning."

Eyes darting from Morrissey to Falken, Keller began trembling. "Y-y-you can't do that."

"Why not?" Falken said.

"Sh-she's innocent."

"How do you know she is?"

"Because I did it." Keller hugged himself and began rocking back and forth. "You are correct, I killed Herr Garrett."

With a sigh of relief, Falken dropped his cigar on the floor and crushed it with his toe. He sat down. "Tell us what happened."

Sobbing, Keller bowed his head and recounted the murder in detail. His version of events mirrored Falken's deductions, with a few minor deviations. He concluded with, "I was afraid of being caught with the body. When I drove onto the bridge, it was raining so hard I couldn't see very far. It seemed unlikely anyone could see me. I wanted it to be finished. So I rolled the body off the bridge, turned the wagon around and went back."

Falken nodded. "What did you do with Garrett's things?"

"I threw everything over the side, except this." Keller pulled a brown wallet from the inside pocket of his jacket and laid it on the table.

Falken picked up the wallet and turned it over. The Garrett House emblem was stamped into the leather. He opened it and withdrew an envelope and a stack of ten-, twenty- and fifty-dollar notes. The envelope, cut open along the top edge, was addressed to Charles. The handwriting had a feminine flourish. He put the envelope and money back inside.

"Why did you do it?"

Keller placed his hands flat on the table and closed his eyes for several seconds. "He took everything from me. Six years of my life, my soul, my ... everything. I was crushed and ruined by his greed. Killing him seemed like just recompense."

"The knife?"

"In the river."

"Garrett's coat?"

"The coat, my soiled clothing, bedsheet and bat are in a gunnysack in the loft of the wagonhouse."

"Did you really cut your hand on a beer bottle?"

"I ... it was dark. I mistakenly picked the knife up by the blade."

Falken nodded. "Captain Morrissey?"

"I'm satisfied."

"Then you'll—"

"Yes, Major, she'll be released immediately."

Falken stood. Westfall packed up the satchel. Keller began crying again.

Falken nodded to Morrissey and offered Gretchen his arm. At first her expression was wary. She looked like a young woman who had spent eighteen hours in jail. Her hair was a mess, her hands were dirty, and her pale blue dress was wrinkled, the hem soiled. Her eyes were dull and bloodshot, and her face was drawn. Falken noted that she smelled like a jailhouse.

With a scornful glare at Morrissey, Gretchen accepted Falken's arm, clung to him. They walked to the jail exit at the rear of the Four Courts Building, with Westfall trailing at a discreet distance.

Outside, the midday sun was bright and hot, and the air was still and heavy with the smoke of thousands of chimneys.

Strolling toward Clark Avenue, Gretchen shaded her eyes, with her free hand. "He didn't say why I've been let go."

"Your name has been cleared. The murderer is in custody."

"Who?"

"Keller. He made a full confession."

"Did he say why he did it?"

"Yes, it seems you were correct. He feels Garrett betrayed him by being human, for having human weakness. So he took his revenge."

"Mein Gott."

"Quite. Man has a regrettable propensity for misdirected violence."

"Luckily we have you to untangle the webs and discover the truth. Thank you, for my freedom and my life."

Falken felt his face flush and swallowed a small lump in his throat. "You are welcome."

They crossed Clark Avenue and continued onto Market Street. Falken struggled with a confused mess of emotions. She reminded him so much of Anna. Just walking with her seemed to relieve the years of torment and anguish. He felt alive again, free. His heart wanted to pursue her, to learn her wants and desires, fantasies and foibles. However, his brain reminded him that she was half his age and pregnant with a bastard child. She had wantonly tried to rob a family of its husband and father. Yet …

They stopped at Market Street. Falken said, "I'll escort you home."

Gretchen withdrew her arm. "That won't be necessary."

"Please, I insist."

Gretchen shook her head. "I look awful, feel filthy, and smell worse. I'm not fit to be in the company of a proper gentleman. Besides, I'm not likely to get a warm reception. You don't deserve to be tainted by association."

The familiar weight returned to Falken's heart. He knew he would not see her again. "At least let me get you a cab." Without waiting for a reply, he hailed a passing hansom. As the driver pulled to the curb, he said, "Adams might not let you in to pack your belongings. Do you still have the card I gave you?"

"Yes." With a coy grin, Gretchen asked, "What does H. H. stand for?"

Falken grinned in reply. "Herbert Herman. Herman was my father."

Gretchen leaned forward and kissed him on the cheek. "God bless you, Herbert Herman Falken." Then she climbed into the cab.

Eyes misty, Falken flipped the driver a half eagle. "Take her wherever she needs to go, as many stops as she may require."

With a disbelieving smile, the driver tipped his hat and replied, "My pleasure, sir."

As the horse clopped away, Westfall stepped forward. "I propose a celebratory lunch."

Falken was watching the cab. "No," he said, "you go on. I have a personal matter to resolve."

"It was just a thought. I'll go on home. I'm sure Mrs. Howard will have something prepared." Westfall rubbed his chin. "Should we expect you for supper?"

The cab turned left at the end of the block and disappeared from sight. Falken nodded and hailed another for himself.

CHAPTER TWENTY-ONE

The next morning, Falken stood before his mirror shaving. He stared into his sad, weary eyes, knowing he had done the right thing but hating himself for it. The memory replayed in his mind, yet again.

He had stood in the Tipperary Social Club parlor, hat in hand, his insides knotted. Sarah walked in, expressionless, and closed the pocket doors. Rather than rushing into his arms and giving him a passionate kiss, she had remained by the doors, arms crossed, shoulders pulled back, head tilted slightly to the left. He called this her I'm-angry-with-you pose.

Her voice had a hard edge. "I trust you're here to apologize."

"Yes, but not for the reasons you expect."

Her eyes narrowed. "Get on with it then."

"I am a fool—"

"You'll get no argument from me on that point."

"I … I thought we could continue as we have been, but I can't go on fooling myself. I've treasured every moment with you. I care for you a great deal, but I don't love you. If I've misled you in any way, I'm sorry."

She drew a sharp breath and suddenly seemed very fragile, as if the slightest movement would shatter her into a thousand pieces. Her face contorted into a mask of shock, fear and sorrow. After several moments, her eyes erupted with fire. Hands on hips, chin thrust out, she said, "Sorry? That's all you have to say? You're *sorry?*"

"Sarah, you must believe I never intended to hurt—"

"Never intended …" She covered her face with both hands and trembled.

"Sarah, please."

She uncovered her face and stabbed a finger at him. "Please *what?* Try to understand? Don't take it so hard? Forgive you?" She spat on the floor. "Shove your apology and your intentions up your arse and take them straight to hell with you." She pointed to the doors. "Get out of here and never come back. *Never.*" Tears began streaming down her cheeks.

He had wanted to say more, but he held his tongue and walked out. Descending the steps to his waiting cab, he heard her call out above him. He turned and looked up.

"Here, you heartless bastard, take your things with you." Clothing, shoes, toiletries, and a small leather bag came flying out Sarah's second-floor window. She stuck her head and shoulders out of the window. "Oh, and don't forget this." She jerked a gold necklace and locket from her neck, a Christmas gift, and flung it down at him. "Bastard!" She retreated from the window. "Bastard!"

Cheeks and ears burning, he retrieved the bag, stuffed his belongings into it, and climbed into the cab. As the horse pulled away, his own tears flowed. *You deserve better than I can offer, Sarah. I'm sorry.*

Finished with his morning routine and dressed for the day, Falken went downstairs to breakfast, although he was not hungry. A rolling rumble reached his ears as he entered the dining room.

"Good morning, Major," said Westfall.

"Good morning, James. Do I hear thunder?" Falken sat and habitually reached for the coffee cup set before him.

Instead of reading the newspaper as usual, Westfall had a leather-bound journal opened on the table. "Yes, I've seen several flashes of lightning, and my leg's killing me."

"Your scarred bones have my sympathy, but I suppose we need the rain. What are you reading?"

"I realize it's unwise to look a gift horse in the mouth, but I can't help myself." Westfall paused for a sip of coffee. "Keller's sudden confession bothers me, so I'm reviewing the case notes, trying to understand why he did it."

Confronted with a new problem, Sarah retreated from Falken's mind. "What do you mean?"

Mrs. Howard entered the dining room with two plates of breakfast. After serving them, she said, "Major, it's none of my business, but you need to do something about this."

Falken looked at her, puzzled.

She crossed her arms and looked down at him as a mother would. "Your insomnia's getting worse. I can tell just by looking at you. If you don't do something, one of these days you're going to go down and not get up again. A body can take only so much before it gives out. Now, I'm a god-fearing woman and I don't say this lightly, but you ought to take a drink or two before bed, just so you can sleep."

"Thank you, Mrs. Howard. I'll ask Dr. Evans if he can prescribe something that doesn't contain spirits. An herbal tea, perhaps."

"You better, or I'll have Mr. James and Luke hold you while I pour some liquor down your throat." She winked, with a mischievous smile.

Morning light shining through the open windows dimmed quickly.

Mrs. Howard looked out the window. "Looks like we're in for a gully washer. Mr. James, keep an eye on those windows." Then she sauntered back to the kitchen.

"Whether you want to hear it or not, she's right," said Westfall.

Falken picked up his fork, the smell of bacon and biscuits reviving his appetite. "What were you saying about Keller?"

A bright flash was followed by a loud crack of thunder, which reverberated through the house.

Digging into his own food, Westfall winced. "Damn, that was close." He glanced over his shoulder at the open windows.

"Keller's behavior doesn't fit," Westfall said. "It seems odd that the plight of an innocent girl would suddenly give a cold-blooded murderer a conscience. I've reread my notes several times. He coolly denied everything, even taunted you, until you mentioned the girl. Then he turned to mush and reversed himself. It just doesn't make sense."

As he ate, Falken recalled the moment of Keller's confession. A glimmer of something began to stir in his mind.

"It's not as if he knows her," Westfall continued. "According to the girl, what she knew of Keller came from Garrett."

Another nearby clap of thunder shuddered through the walls.

The glimmer in Falken's mind became a speck of something. His brain scratched at it, trying to uncover its shape and definition.

"But when you said her name ..."

Falken didn't hear the rest of Westfall's words. With a forkful of egg halfway to his mouth, he saw Sarah's eyes when he said he didn't love her. That image was replaced by Keller's eyes at the moment the man had spoken Gretchen's name. He compared one to the other, as if examining photographs side by side.

It can't be, he thought. But it was. Both wore expressions of heartbreak. He struggled to accept this realization as another thought began taking shape.

"Major? Major?"

Falken's eyes refocused on his empty fork, and egg on the tablecloth. "Yes?"

"I asked if you're all right." Westfall was sitting down after closing the windows. Large raindrops pelted the glass panes, while lightning flashed and thunder rolled across the sky.

Falken put down his fork. "No, I'm not." He stroked his mustache while his brain churned. He knew he was missing something, small yet significant. It was the little things, always the little things. Slivers and splinters of thoughts overlooked and discarded. Wait. What was that? Slivers and splinters. Discarded splinters. What was it she'd said?

Falken held out his hand. "Give me the journal."

"What is it?"

"The journal, please."

Westfall handed it over, and Falken flipped through the pages. There.

"I dropped the broken bat and tried to go to him."

He turned more pages. Neither Westfall's description of the private room nor his diagram indicated a broken bat on the floor. Next he turned to Garrett's confession, running his finger down the pages. There.

"The knife?"

"In the river."

"Garrett's coat?"

"The coat, my soiled clothing, bedsheet and bat are in a gunnysack in the loft of the wagon house."

He moved his finger back up the page. Yes, Keller kept the wallet and her love letter to Garrett.

"He took everything from me. Six years of my youth, my soul, my ... everything. I was crushed and ruined by his greed."

"Major, please tell me what you've found."

"Why did Keller take the bat?"

"Bat?"

"The baseball bat Gretchen hit Garrett with. Why did Keller take it from the room? It wasn't of any consequence to him. So why remove the pieces and hide them?"

Falken read the relevant excerpts aloud for Westfall's benefit.

Westfall's face screwed up in thought as he chewed. Moments later, he said, "He was protecting her. He was protecting her … when he confessed. But why?"

Falken pushed back from the table. "He threw everything away, except the wallet. It contained her love letter to another man." He shook a finger at the ceiling as a deep bass peal of thunder rattled the windows. "He protected her because he loves her. He knew she was Garrett's mistress. That's why he murdered him. He took revenge on the man who stole his love. The man who 'took everything' from him."

"Is there something else?"

"I'm not sure, but I want to find that bat."

"Captain Morrissey should have it."

"Why would he even look? He has a confession, his job is done."

"Why is it so important?"

Falken shook his head. "It may not be, but I want to find it anyway."

Westfall looked over his shoulder at the raging storm outside. "Do we have to go now?"

"Yes, telephone for a cab to pick us up."

Westfall nodded, shoveled potatoes into his mouth, then hobbled out.

Falken stood and crossed to the kitchen door. Poking his head in, he said, "Owen, finish your breakfast and get dressed. We're going out."

Mrs. Howard turned from the sink. "Major, you can't go out in this weather. If you don't get struck by lightning, you'll drown."

"When duty calls, men must answer."

"Uh-huh." Mrs. Howard stared holes through Falken. "But *men* won't be answering any calls to duty from a hospital bed or the cemetery." Shaking her head, she turned back to the sink and muttered to herself.

Falken nodded to Owen and withdrew.

CHAPTER TWENTY-TWO

Falken and Westfall dug through mounds of hay and straw in the wagonhouse loft. Owen was below, feeding and watering the horses; apparently the stablehands had stopped coming to work as well. All three men were dripping, hay and straw was stuck to their wet clothing, and manure caked their shoes. Outside, a steady rain continued falling.

After thirty minutes of sweaty work with a pitchfork, Falken paused to catch his breath. He craved a cigar, but suppressed the desire. *The last thing I need is an arson charge*, he thought.

Westfall, working furiously with a rake several feet away, also stopped and took several deep breaths. "We're not looking for a needle, but still." Then he looked down at himself. "This suit will never come clean, and we're chasing our tails. Damn Keller!" He threw the rake to the floor and kicked the hay in front of him with his good leg. His foot struck something.

"What's that?" Falken said, and rushed over.

Both men dug into the pile with their hands. Falken touched coarse fabric and pulled a gunnysack free.

Grinning, Westfall said, "I was beginning to think he lied about it."

Falken upended the sack. A mildewed coat, bloodstained bedsheet, clothing, and a baseball bat fell to the floor. They stared in disbelief.

"It's not broken," Westfall said.

Falken picked up the bat. Dried blood on the worn chipped barrel was clearly visible.

"But why would she lie about breaking the bat?" Westfall said.

Falken's heart sank. She couldn't, he thought. She's so young. So much like Anna. He stared at the blood for several seconds, picturing Gretchen crying and Anna falling. He had thought that saving Gretchen from Morrissey was a sort of redemption for Anna's death, but …

"Major?"

"I don't know why she lied, so we must ask her."

"Do you think she's at Garrett's?"

Falken dropped to one knee and stuffed the clothing, coat, sheet, and bat back into the sack. An image of Keller's baggage flashed into his mind. "Keller was leaving the city with no intention of returning. He had everything he owns packed up and ready to go."

"Yes, he was going to Milwaukee."

"Was he?" Falken stood and stroked his mustache. "If you're a murderer trying to bluff your way past a police captain, do you reveal your true destination?"

"Well, if not Milwaukee, where else would he be going?"

"Yes, where?"

Falken stood, picked up the bag and started toward the stairs. The thoughts swirling in his head stabbed him deeply, and made him question himself. Had he allowed his personal guilt to cloud his professional judgment? Was he a professional, or an annoying amateur finally exposed as such? Was his sleep-deprived brain fit to make judgments about culpability and innocence?

At the bottom of the stairs, he called out to Owen.

The young orderly approached and said, "I've done what I can for the poor beasts." He pointed to the sack. "You found it?"

"Yes. Now we need to brush each other off and make ourselves presentable. We have to see a man about a train."

Bits of hay and straw still clinging to his sodden suit and favorite black homburg, Falken walked up to the ticket counter. Men, women and children bustled through the concourse of Union Station's headhouse. Excited boys and girls chased each other; harried mothers demanded obedience; porters toted loads of baggage, large and small; several vagrants moved around, begging pennies and nickels; vendors moved through the crowd, hawking refreshments, cigarettes and newspapers.

A balding, bespectacled ticket clerk with a bored expression looked up. "Destination, sir?"

"When did the last train for San Francisco depart?" Falken asked.

"Eleven o'clock yesterday morning."

"And when will the next one leave?"

"Eleven o'clock."

Falken pulled out his watch and opened it: ten-twenty. "When will boarding begin?"

"Half past."

"And which track?"

"Seven. Do you want to purchase a ticket?"

"No, thank you." Falken turned away.

He rejoined Westfall and Owen, explained what he had learned, and added, "We'll take up position on the midway, near the gate to track seven. Owen, you haven't met Miss Heinen, so listen carefully." He provided the young man with a detailed description.

They moved off, with Owen carrying the gunnysack.

Westfall hobbled along with his cane and satchel. "How do you know she's going to board this train, Major?"

"I don't," Falken said, "but this is where my instincts point."

"What do we do if she took yesterday's train?" Owen asked.

"She was still in jail when it departed," Falken replied. "This is her first opportunity to flee the city."

"*If* she plans to run, and *if* she plans to run west," Westfall said.

"We'll know soon enough."

Union Station was the main waypoint for travel west of the Mississippi River. The midway was crowded with arriving and departing passengers, and those welcoming them or waving goodbye. A cross section of America moved to and fro: industrialists, bankers, merchants, soldiers, sailors, entrepreneurs, engineers, laborers, ranchers and farmers; rich and poor, privileged and common, educated and illiterate, natural born and immigrant, old and young.

Under the train shed, locomotives hissed steam while hot iron popped and creaked, and sooty black smoke rose from the stacks. Conductors called out to passengers and each other. Firemen tended their boilers, while engineers inspected couplers and brake lines.

Falken took the center position, before the train shed gate for track seven, with his companions several feet to either side. At half past ten, travelers began streaming toward the gate, interspersed with grunting, sweating porters. He scanned every female face as the crowd diverted around him. A couple of times a minute, he glanced at Westfall and Owen.

As the minutes ticked by, Falken shifted from one foot to the other and frequently checked his watch, vacillating between a compulsion to spot Gretchen and the hope that he would not. He lit a cigar and drew contemplatively. She hadn't done anything wrong beyond lying about the bat. She might yet be innocent. But one thing was clear: no matter how much he wished that she was Anna, she wasn't Anna and never would be. There would never be another Anna. She was gone forever, and he had to accept it.

He sighed, fought back tears and maintained his vigil.

Five minutes to go. Falken snapped his watch closed and stuffed it back in his vest pocket with a sense of failure. He resisted an urge to pace back and forth. Damn, he thought, she's slipped away. Probably—

He saw a flash of blonde hair bobbing through the crowd. A second later, he caught another glimpse between the milling bodies. He rose onto the balls of his feet and moved his head from side to side. Where did she go? He wanted to yell at everyone on the midway to get out of the way. She had been coming this way, but now he couldn't see her. Damn, why wouldn't these people move along?

Falken took two steps to the left and craned his neck. Nothing. Then he sidestepped to the right. It might not have been—

Two men stepped aside, and Gretchen Heinen passed between them. She was walking quickly, a brown leather satchel in her right hand, a homemade drawstring purse in her left. A porter trailed her carrying two large suitcases. When she was within ten feet, Falken advanced and intercepted her.

"Good morning, Miss Heinen."

Gretchen stopped abruptly. Her expression switched rapidly from confusion to recognition, then uncertainty. "Good morning, Herbert. What are you doing here?"

"I'm looking for you. A question has come up that requires an answer. But first I have to ask, where did you get that satchel?"

Gretchen glanced down. "It belonged to my father."

The scuffed and frayed satchel had been part of Keller's luggage. Lie number two.

"Leaving town?"

Gretchen glanced right and left as Westfall and Owen came alongside. "Yes, a sick friend needs my help."

Falken nodded. "Where does your sick friend live?"

"Kansas City."

"Really? I hope it's not serious." Lie number three.

"Herbert, I don't have time to chat." Gretchen pointed beyond him. "My train's leaving in the next few minutes."

"Oh, you have time. There's another train to Kansas City this afternoon, and still another in the evening."

Gretchen moved to her right and started forward. "I'm sorry, Herbert, but I must go."

Falken closed in and grasped her upper left arm. "I think not."

Gretchen frowned. "Let go of my arm. You're hurting me." She looked around, "*Hilfe! Help!* This man is hurting me."

The porter put down the bags and seemed to be weighing the wisdom of interfering with a white man's business.

Tightening his grip, Falken turned to Owen. "Find a policeman," he said, "and be quick about it."

As Owen strode away, the porter clasped his hands behind his back and waited, suspicious eyes on Falken.

Gretchen struggled to free herself and continued to call out. "Someone, please help me."

A crowd of gawkers gathered quickly.

A short pudgy man said to Falken, "What're you doing to that girl? Let go of her."

Westfall moved in and took hold of Gretchen's right arm to still her movements. "This could turn ugly, Major."

Another Good Samaritan joined the pudgy man. "You heard him. Release that young lady this instant."

An unseen voice cried, "Somebody call a cop."

"Please, they're hurting me," Gretchen continued.

As the pair of saviors stepped forward, Owen returned with a police sergeant in tow. The sergeant pushed through the crowd and surveyed the scene.

"Oh, it's you, Major Falken," he said. "What's going on?"

Excited murmurs rose from the onlookers:

"Major Falken."

"It's Major Falken."

The pudgy man and his partner faded back into the crowd. The porter nodded and continued watching with interest.

"Sergeant, I want you to arrest this woman," Falken said.

The sergeant looked Gretchen up and down with an appraising expression. "If you say so, Major." Rubbing his chin, he asked, "What's the charge?"

"Murder."

CHAPTER TWENTY-THREE

With the police sergeant in the lead, Falken and company escorted Gretchen back to the Four Courts, interrogation room two. She had not uttered a sound since leaving Union Station.

Captain Morrissey came up behind them. "What're you doing, Major?" He pointed at the ceiling. "Keller's upstairs being charged right now. And where have you been? You're soaked through."

"Keller's about to be joined by a co-defendant," Falken replied.

"But you—"

"It'll all make sense in a few minutes. Please join us."

Shaking his head, Morrissey threw up his hands and followed Falken into the room. "What have you been up to? You smell like a stable and look like you've been rolling around in one."

The sergeant seated Gretchen, clapped the manacles on her wrists, and moved to the adjacent corner. Westfall arranged himself at the writing desk.

Owen set the satchel, purse, and gunnysack on the table and withdrew to a corner. Falken stood across from Gretchen, while Morrissey leaned against the wall behind him.

Falken placed his hands on the chair back and said, "A number of lies and half-truths have been told this past week. Today we're going to expose the whole truth of Charles Garrett's murder." He made eye contact with Gretchen. "And your part in it." Her gaze was cold and steady. "You told us you argued with Garrett and broke a baseball bat over his head because you were scared."

He paused for a moment. "Keller didn't throw the bat in the river. He told us where he hid it, and we found it." He picked up the sack and pulled out the bat. "As you can see, it has blood on it," he said, pointing to the stain, "but it's not broken."

Gretchen's eyes and nostrils flared, but she remained silent.

"There's no reason I can think of for you to lie about this particular detail, so I must conclude that you believed the bat was indeed broken." Falken laid the bat and sack back on the table, and took his time lighting a cigar.

Gretchen stared at the bat with disbelief. She squirmed on the chair, lightly rattling the manacle chains. She did not speak, shed tears, or tremble.

"The logical explanation is that Keller lied to you," Falken said. "He used the bat to stun Garrett before attacking with the knife. After all, he was facing a man twice his size and needed an advantage. When it was over he came out and, for whatever reason, told you the bat had broken. Why did you claim that you hit him?"

In reply, Gretchen offered an angry defiant stare and continued silence.

Falken shrugged and blew smoke in her face. "Next you claim to be en route to Kansas City to visit a sick friend. Yet you told me you have no family or friends in America. No one to turn to in your time of need, is what you said. Also, you said you don't have any money. If your friend is real, which I doubt, how did you pay for the ticket?"

Silence.

Falken picked up Gretchen's purse, pulled the top open, and dumped its contents on the table. There was a handkerchief embroidered with Garrett's monogram, a train ticket, a coin purse, and a straight razor. He grasped the razor and held it up.

"I'm told prostitutes carry these for self-defense." He put it down well out of her reach then selected the ticket. He examined it and whistled appreciatively. "First class to San Francisco, three hundred dollars. Quite a sum for a pregnant, soon-to-be-destitute parlormaid."

Dropping the ticket on the table, he grabbed the coin purse and opened it.

This time, Owen whistled as Falken pulled out a thick wad of bank notes, a large handful of gold and silver coins, and a key. He counted while sorting the money into piles by denomination.

"I make it one hundred eighty-seven dollars in small bills, one hundred ten in gold, and about five dollars in silver, minus the three hundred you paid at the ticket counter. That's a little over six hundred dollars. Where did you get it?" He drew on the cigar and blew a smoke ring. "Were you blackmailing Garrett yourself, or working for Devlin?"

Morrissey interrupted. "Major, isn't that the same case we saw at Keller's?"

"Yes, I believe it is. Miss Heinen must have retrieved it yesterday, after I so brilliantly secured her release from your jail."

"I'd like to see what's in it," Morrissey said.

"So would I." Falken pulled the satchel across the table and tugged on the locked hasp. After a moment, he picked up the key from the table and fitted it into the lock. With a twist, the lock opened and he pulled back the top flap.

Peering over Falken's shoulder, Morrissey said, "Jesus, Mary and Joseph. There's a king's ransom in there."

For a moment, Falken stared in disbelief. Then he began pulling bundles of bank notes of all denominations from the full satchel.

He counted the pile twice. "Forty thousand dollars." Locking eyes with Gretchen, he said, "Did Devlin pay you this money, or did you steal it?"

All eyes were on Gretchen. She looked around the room, spat on the floor, and cocked her head to the right. "Work for that Irish *Schweinehund*? I wouldn't piss on his grave."

"Then where did you get this money?"

"From Charles," Gretchen replied, with a self-satisfied grin.

"Garrett? He was bankrupt. It's the one thing everyone agrees on."

Gretchen shook her head. "Charles began hiding money from Devlin, and everyone else, immediately. I wasn't even supposed to know. It was his stake for the future. He knew he was going to lose everything. So, like a good businessman, he planned ahead. His talk about a life for us in San Francisco was all lies. He was using me for his own pleasure and intended to leave me behind when they moved on."

"Moved on?" Falken said.

"He was going to move his wife and her brats to Little Rock and start a new brewery after his bankers and creditors seized everything."

"How did you discover this?"

"Franz. He's been smitten with me for some time. Charles used him to hide it." Gretchen nodded at the pile of cash. "He had to be in on the scheme because Devlin was going to Garrett House and inspecting the ledgers at least twice a week. He intended to squeeze every penny out of Charles. Franz knew about our affair, but wanted me for himself. So he told me everything."

"So, while Garrett was stringing you along, you did the same to Keller. What did you promise Keller to convince him to murder Garrett?"

Gretchen shook her head. "Franz planned the murder. Stealing the money was also his idea. My job was to leave the door open, that's all. He said that afterward we'd go to Milwaukee, start a business and live happily ever after."

"You actually expect us to believe that?"

"Believe what you will, Herbert." Gretchen fixed Falken with a steely gaze. "Men have been using me since I sprouted these." Chains rattling, she cupped a breast in each hand. Matter-of-factly, she added, "Just once, I wanted to get something out of it. Franz was my opportunity." Her hands fell back to her lap.

Falken waved his cigar at her dismissively. "What about the bat?"

"Franz said my story would be more believable and sympathetic if I admitted to hurting Charles. When he came back out, he was bleeding. I asked what happened, and he said the bat splintered and gouged his hand. Then he told me to go home." Gretchen rolled her eyes. "I had no reason to doubt him."

"Nor, apparently, did you think he would clean up after himself. But for that," Falken said, indicating the baseball bat with his chin, "you would've gotten away and left Keller to face justice alone."

"Franz is good with numbers, but otherwise he's a simple-minded fool. Eventually he would've found some way of putting his head in a noose."

Falken drew on his cigar. "Captain Morrissey?"

"Yes, I have a question. Are you really pregnant?"

Gretchen nodded. "I've been absent the curse for three months."

"Who's the father?"

"I don't know. At times, I had both of them on the same day."

Morrissey nodded to his sergeant. "Take her to lockup and write your arrest report. I'll inform the prosecutor."

As the sergeant was unlocking the manacles, Westfall said, "I'd like to ask a question." Everyone looked at him. "Who was responsible for the shooting?"

Face contorted in confusion, Gretchen asked, "What shooting?"

CHAPTER TWENTY-FOUR

The next morning, Falken stood near the spot where the bodies of Charles Garrett and Anna Schrader had lain on the riverbank, fifteen years apart. The heavy rain had once again cleaned the air, but also washed a load of stinking runoff into the Mississippi. A mixture of foul odors rising out of the steadily flowing water stung his nose. A northbound steamboat, sidewheels churning brown water, passed under Eads Bridge; an eastbound train chugged and clattered above, smoke billowing out from the rail deck.

He stared at a spot in the steamboat's wake, the place where Anna appeared in his dreams. He whispered, "I'm so sorry I let go of your hands. I'm sorry I didn't save you." Tears streamed down his cheeks.

I loved you more than anything in this world. I still do and always will. But my feelings for you have blinded me. Guilt clouded my good judgment. I've been so desperate to have you back I latched onto a surrogate, a despicable murderess I nearly set free. I willingly fell under her spell, and for that I'm ashamed. This is not fair; we both know life rarely is, but I cannot allow myself to commit such foolish errors again. You will always be in my heart, but I must put you out of my mind. For the good of the living people who depend on me, I must. If we meet again, I hope you can forgive me. Until then, I love you. Goodbye.

Falken pulled a monogrammed silk handkerchief from his breast pocket and wiped his eyes. To his surprise, he felt a great weight disappear; the familiar tightness of his chest lessened; his mind seemed clearer; the turbulent storm of emotions he carried within seemed to calm. He breathed deeply and savored his moment of, at least partial, liberation.

After several minutes, he turned away from the river and climbed the levee.

Crossing the railroad tracks, Falken stopped abruptly as a tingle ran down his spine. He stopped between the center tracks and looked around; he twisted and turned, shifting his gaze upstream, downstream, across the river toward East St. Louis, at nearby windows and rooftops. *Where the hell are you? Who are you? Why are you following me?*

After a minute, a familiar figure appeared atop the bridge embankment and waved. His sensation of being watched unabated, Falken moved off again.

When they were within arm's reach, Morrissey said, "What're you doing here?"

"Something I should have done a long time ago," Falken replied, slightly winded. "What are *you* doing here?"

"Thought you'd like to know she'll be charged Monday morning. The prosecutor's recommending twenty years for her, and the gallows for Keller. Judge Lambert will approve the sentences."

"She'll be just shy of forty upon her release, still young enough to chase her pot of gold by duping another man. Are they squeamish about hanging a woman?"

"Keller won't say a word against her," Morrissey said, "and I can't put blood on her hands. The prosecutor says he won't hang her for being an accomplice, says hanging a woman without irrefutable proof of actual murder won't look good in the newspapers."

"She was the mastermind and manipulated him at every turn. You were right about her all along." Falken glanced over his shoulder at the river. "I just didn't see it."

"Never mind about that, Major, you got it right in the end." Morrissey removed his helmet and scratched his head, frowning. "There's something else."

Falken arched an eyebrow.

"I questioned both of them, even got a little rough. They claim to be ignorant of the shooting."

"Do you believe them?"

"Yes. I doubt either knows how to load a rifle, let alone fire one at long range. And I got the prosecutor to offer lighter sentences if they identified the shooter. The girl would've given the orders and damn sure would've jumped on the chance to save herself ten years. It wasn't them. A while ago I had another run at the chink. He still swears Devlin and his boys never left." Morrissey's eyes stated he had gotten a little rough with the Chinaman as well.

With the feeling of being watched still strong, Falken accepted the news without comment.

"Do you have any idea who it might be?" Morrissey asked.

Falken shook his head.

"You still armed?"

"Yes." Falken patted his jacket pocket. "Is the money being released to Mrs. Garrett, or passed onto creditors?"

"The mortgage on the home and furnishings will be paid Monday, along with the household accounts. The rest goes to whoever grabs it first."

"At least Mrs. Garrett will be able to sell the house."

"If she's smart, they can buy a smaller home and live on what's left until one of the daughters marries."

They walked over to the waiting police carriage. Morrissey said, "Offer you a ride? See that you get home alive?"

Falken shook his head. "No, I'm going to walk around for awhile. I refuse to cower and live in fear."

"Suit yourself." Morrissey climbed aboard. Once seated, he leaned out the door and added, "Oh, by the way, are you going to the fights tonight?"

"I haven't given it any thought. Why?"

"My bookmaker tells me the line on you is eight to one, if you decide to show up."

"Really?"

Morrissey nodded. "O'Donnell's boasting to everyone who'll listen that he's brought a big Polack over from the East Side. Says you're guaranteed to lose if you decide to fight."

"Is that so?"

Morrissey nodded again. "Think I'll go right now and put down a double eagle this time, just in case."

"A police captain wagering on bare knuckle fights? I'm appalled."

"Good day, Major." Morrissey winked and his carriage began rolling.

Falken weaved through the crowd of spectators and bettors. Cheers and groans, directed at the ad-hoc boxing ring, erupted every few seconds. He spotted the green-shaded lantern and headed for it.

As the hoots and howls reached a crescendo, heralding the end of a fight, Falken stood before Seamus O'Donnell. The bookmaker and organizer of the Saturday-night spectacles received a signal from one of his men; a wide smile indicated the outcome.

Falken stepped forward. "Hello, O'Donnell."

The bookmaker looked up, and his eyes sparkled. "So you're not a coward after all. I was ready to start laying bets that you wouldn't show your face."

"Want a chance to win your money back?" Falken extended his right hand, which held five double eagles.

Eyes wide, O'Donnell replied, "That's quite a wager."

"Afraid you'll lose and have to pay out again?"

O'Donnell's eyes narrowed and his wrinkled face furrowed. "It's a bet."

"Eight-to-one odds, correct?"

"No, I'm making the line on you ten to one." O'Donnell sneered. "My beast is going to rip you apart."

"In that case, I'll double my bet," Falken said with a wry grin.

ABOUT THE AUTHOR

Michael Scheffel lives near Fort Leonard Wood, Missouri, with his partner Christine and her daughter Valerie. When the dogs and cat allow him a moment or two, Michael pursues his passion for writing with enthusiasm. He also travels the United States extensively for his other job.

For more information about Michael and his books, to contact him, or enter the monthly draw for a chance to win a signed copy of one of his books, visit his website:

www.michaelscheffel.com

You can also follow Michael on Facebook:
www.facebook.com/michaelscheffel

or Twitter:
@ScheffelMichael